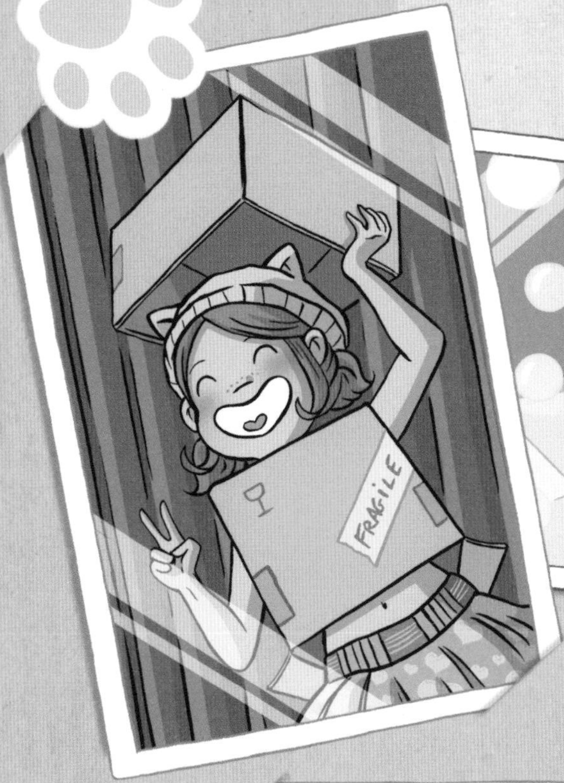
FRAGILE

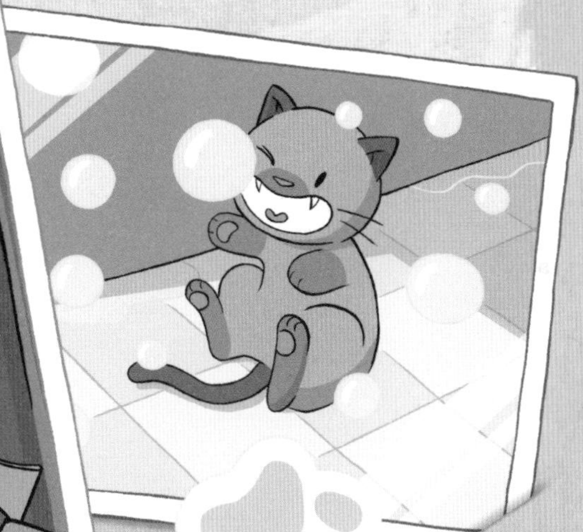

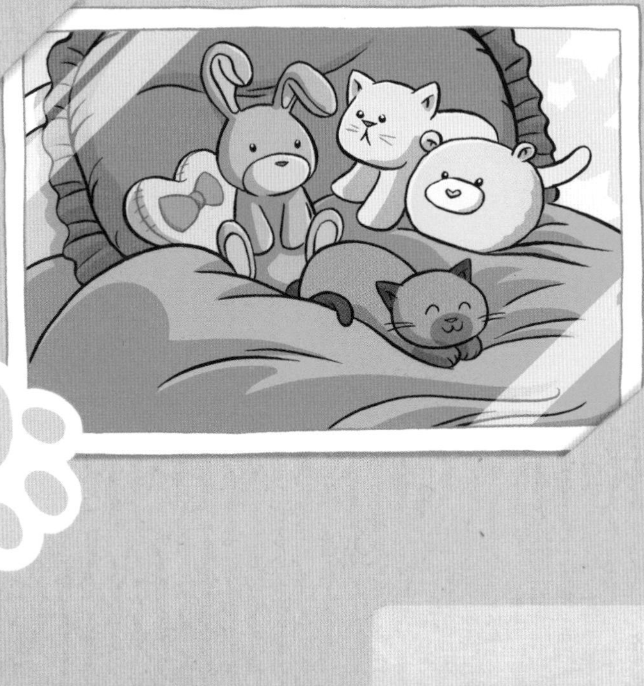

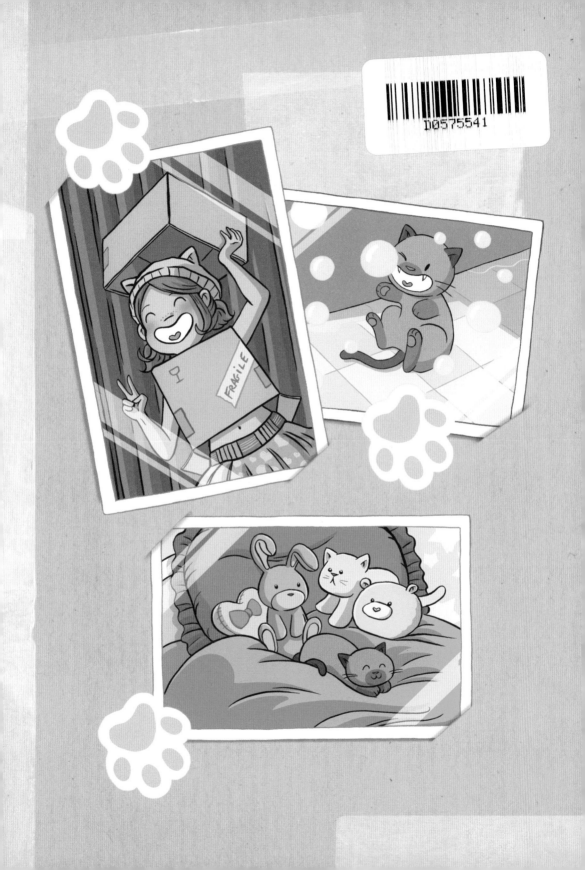

Chloe & Cartoon

...

charmz™

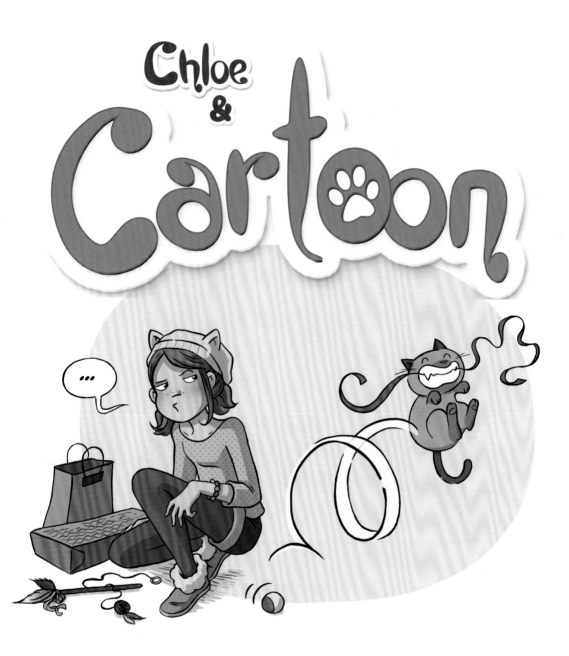

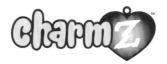

MORE GRAPHIC NOVELS AVAILABLE FROM charmz™

Véronique Grisseaux
Laëtitia Aynié
Amy's Diary
Space Alien... Almost?
India Desjardins
charmz

AMY'S DIARY #1
"SPACE ALIEN... ALMOST?"

Véronique Grisseaux
Laëtitia Aynié
Amy's Diary
The World's Upside Down
India Desjardins
charmz

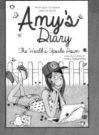

AMY'S DIARY #2
"THE WORLD'S UPSIDE DOWN"

Véronique Grisseaux
Laëtitia Aynié
Amy's Diary
Moving On
India Desjardins
charmz

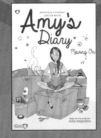

AMY'S DIARY #3
"MOVING ON"

STITCHED
The First Day of the Rest of her Life
charmz

STITCHED #1
"THE FIRST DAY OF THE REST OF HER LIFE"

STITCHED
MARIAH McCOURT - AARON ALEXOVICH
Love in the Time of Assumption
charmz

STITCHED #2
"LOVE IN THE TIME OF ASSUMPTION"

Greg Tessier and Amandine
Chloe
The New Girl
charmz

CHLOE #1
"THE NEW GIRL"

Greg Tessier and Amandine
Chloe
The Queen of High School
charmz

CHLOE #2 "THE QUEEN OF HIGH SCHOOL"

Chloe
Frenemies
charmz

CHLOE #3
"FRENEMIES"

Chloe
Rainy Day
charmz

CHLOE #4
"RAINY DAY"

Ana
COSMIC RACE
THE RACE BEGINS
charmz

ANA AND THE COSMIC RACE #1
"THE RACE BEGINS"

PATRICIA LYFOUNG
The Scarlet Rose
charmz

SCARLET ROSE #1
"I KNEW I'D MEET YOU"

PATRICIA LYFOUNG
The Scarlet Rose
I'll Go Where You Go

SCARLET ROSE #2
"I'LL GO WHERE YOU GO"

PATRICIA LYFOUNG
The Scarlet Rose
I Think I Love You

SCARLET ROSE #3
"I THINK I LOVE YOU"

PATRICIA LYFOUNG
The Scarlet Rose
charmz

SCARLET ROSE #4
"YOU WILL ALWAYS BE MINE"

GFFs
GHOST FRIENDS FOREVER
charmz

G.F.F.s #1
"MY HEART LIES IN THE 90s"

GFFs
GHOST FRIENDS FOREVER
WITCHES GET THINGS DONE
charmz

G.F.F.s #2
"WITCHES GET THINGS DONE"

Monica
WHO CAN AFFORD THE PRICE OF FRIENDSHIP TODAY?!
charmz

MONICA ADVENTURES #1

Monica
We Fought Each Other as Kids... Now We're in Love?!
charmz

MONICA ADVENTURES #2

Monica
Who's Saying Nasty Things About Me...Online?!
charmz

MONICA ADVENTURES #3

Sweeties
CHERRY SKYE
charmz

SWEETIES #1
"CHERRY SKYE"

SEE MORE AT PAPERCUTZ.COM

Cartoon

#1: When Chloe First Met Her Cat, Cartoon

Story by
Greg Tessier

Art by
Amandine

New York

To Cartoon (the real one!), as well as the other little balls of fur who preceded and followed him, true sources of daily happiness. And to all our little playmates who, much to our enjoyment, never fail to surprise us!
- Greg

To my beautiful Sacha, for being such a perfect muse and for so nonchalantly lending his traits
(and his unrivaled portliness!) to Cartoon.
And to Prunelle, Virgule, Lavande, and Meguy-Chérie, obviously!
To Châtaigne and Myrtille, the first camping kitties who, I hope, will bring much happiness to their fabulous owner.
- Amandine

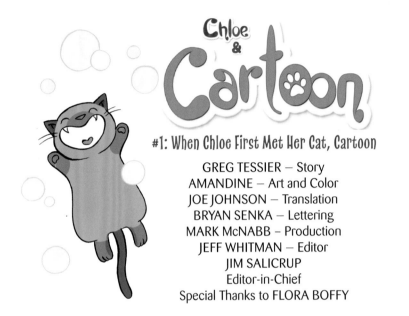

Chloe & Cartoon

#1: When Chloe First Met Her Cat, Cartoon

GREG TESSIER — Story
AMANDINE — Art and Color
JOE JOHNSON — Translation
BRYAN SENKA — Lettering
MARK McNABB — Production
JEFF WHITMAN — Editor
JIM SALICRUP
Editor-in-Chief
Special Thanks to FLORA BOFFY

Mistinguette [CHLOE] & Cartoon volume 1 *"Chat Arrive!"* © Jungle! 2017 and Mistinguette [CHLOE] & Cartoon volume 2 *"Deuxième Chat Pitre"* © Jungle! 2018
www.editions-jungle.com. All rights reserved. Used under license.

English translation and all other editorial material © 2020 by Papercutz. All rights reserved.

Charmz is an imprint of Papercutz.

Charmz books may be purchased for business or promotional use.
For information on bulk purchases please contact Macmillan Corporate and Premium Sales Department at
(800) 221-7945 x5442

Hardcover ISBN: 978-1-5458-0430-8
Paperback ISBN: 978-1-5458-0431-5

Printed in Turkey
February 2020

Distributed by Macmillan
First Charmz Printing

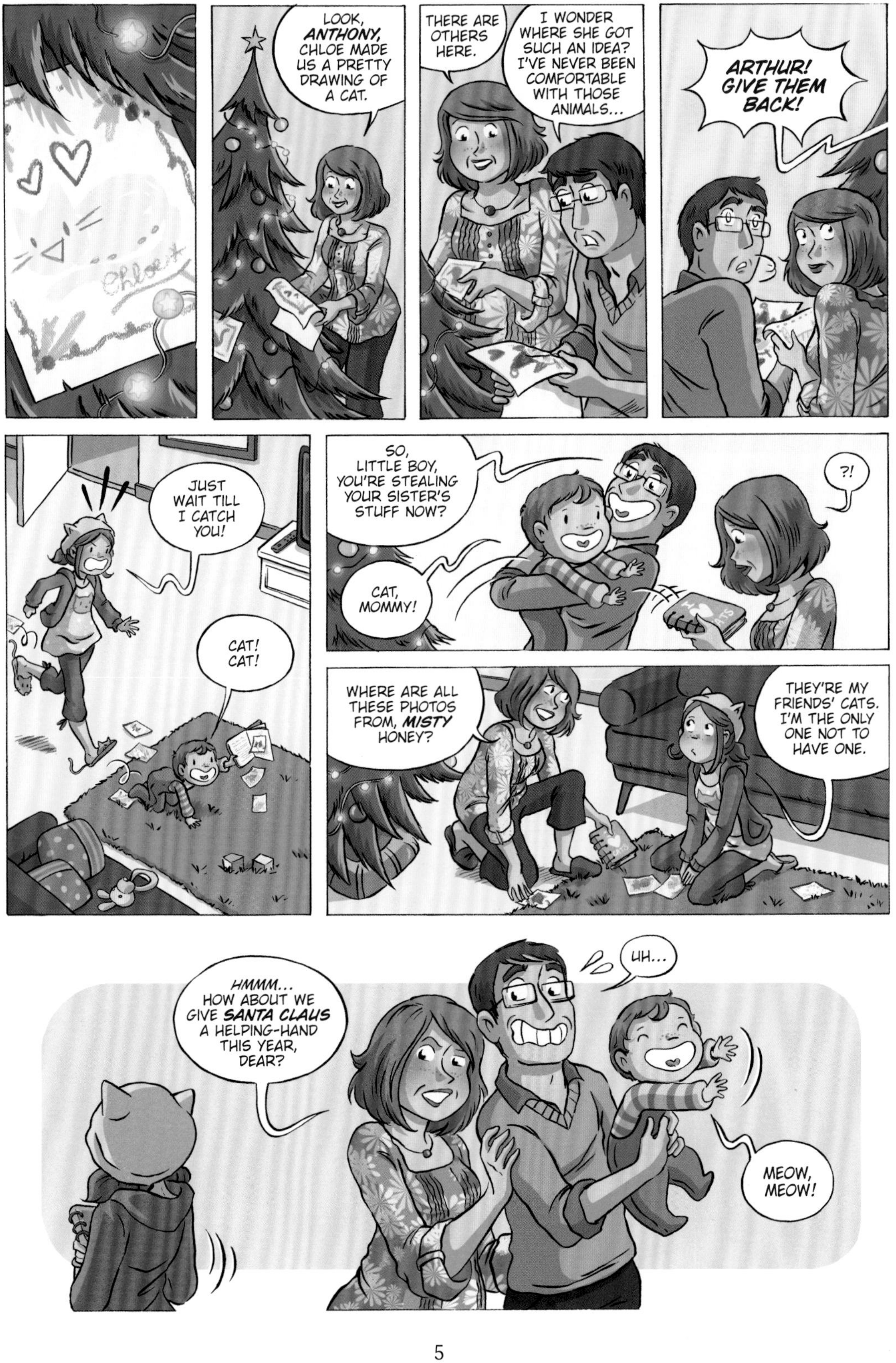
LOOK, ANTHONY, CHLOE MADE US A PRETTY DRAWING OF A CAT.
THERE ARE OTHERS HERE.
I WONDER WHERE SHE GOT SUCH AN IDEA? I'VE NEVER BEEN COMFORTABLE WITH THOSE ANIMALS...
ARTHUR! GIVE THEM BACK!
JUST WAIT TILL I CATCH YOU!
CAT! CAT!
SO, LITTLE BOY, YOU'RE STEALING YOUR SISTER'S STUFF NOW?
CAT, MOMMY!
?!
WHERE ARE ALL THESE PHOTOS FROM, MISTY HONEY?
THEY'RE MY FRIENDS' CATS. I'M THE ONLY ONE NOT TO HAVE ONE.
HMMM... HOW ABOUT WE GIVE SANTA CLAUS A HELPING-HAND THIS YEAR, DEAR?
UH...
MEOW, MEOW!

First Contact

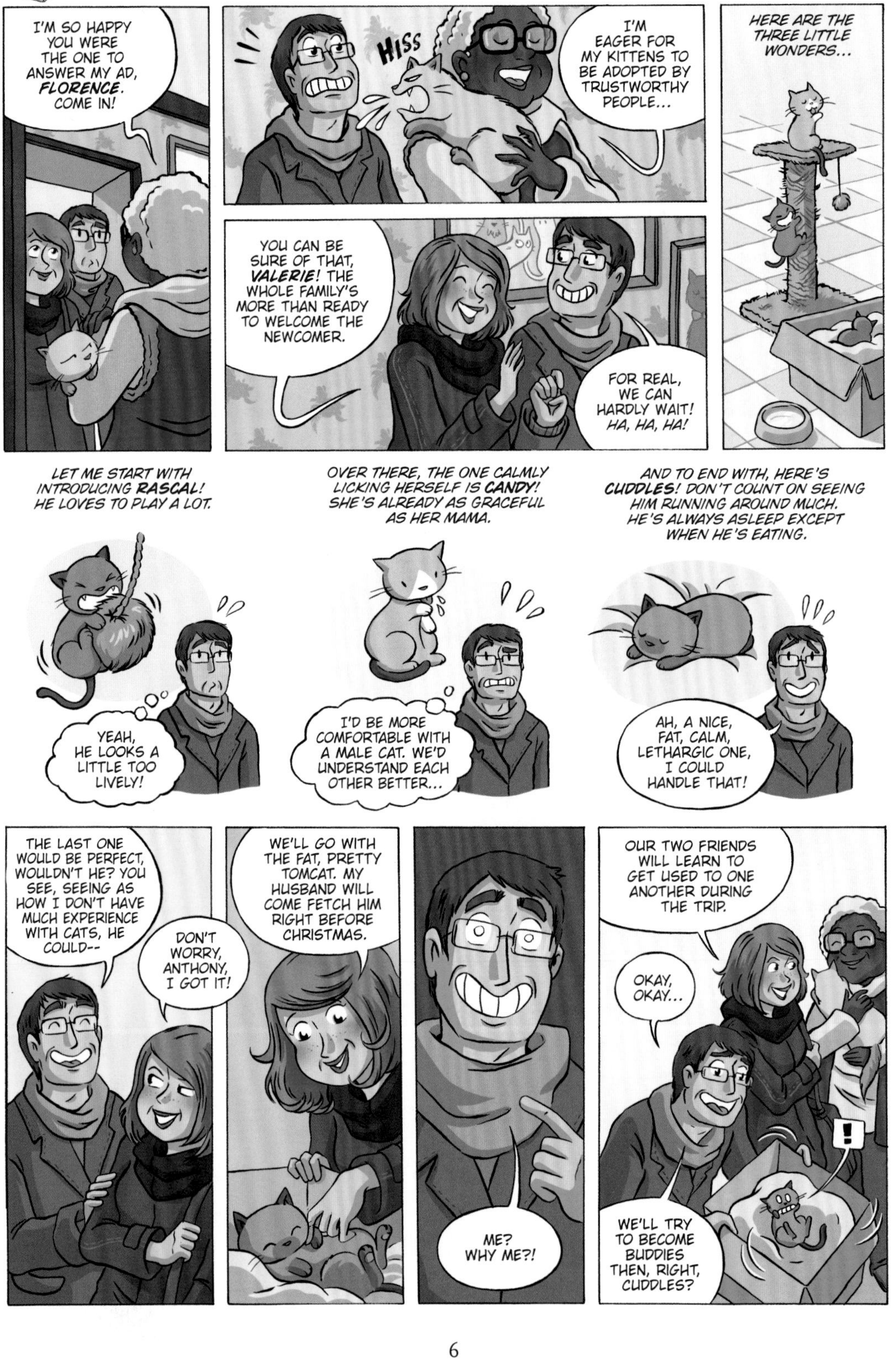

I'M SO HAPPY YOU WERE THE ONE TO ANSWER MY AD, FLORENCE. COME IN!
HISS
I'M EAGER FOR MY KITTENS TO BE ADOPTED BY TRUSTWORTHY PEOPLE...
YOU CAN BE SURE OF THAT, VALERIE! THE WHOLE FAMILY'S MORE THAN READY TO WELCOME THE NEWCOMER.
FOR REAL, WE CAN HARDLY WAIT! HA, HA, HA!
HERE ARE THE THREE LITTLE WONDERS...
LET ME START WITH INTRODUCING RASCAL! HE LOVES TO PLAY A LOT.
YEAH, HE LOOKS A LITTLE TOO LIVELY!
OVER THERE, THE ONE CALMLY LICKING HERSELF IS CANDY! SHE'S ALREADY AS GRACEFUL AS HER MAMA.
I'D BE MORE COMFORTABLE WITH A MALE CAT. WE'D UNDERSTAND EACH OTHER BETTER...
AND TO END WITH, HERE'S CUDDLES! DON'T COUNT ON SEEING HIM RUNNING AROUND MUCH. HE'S ALWAYS ASLEEP EXCEPT WHEN HE'S EATING.
AH, A NICE, FAT, CALM, LETHARGIC ONE, I COULD HANDLE THAT!
THE LAST ONE WOULD BE PERFECT, WOULDN'T HE? YOU SEE, SEEING AS HOW I DON'T HAVE MUCH EXPERIENCE WITH CATS, HE COULD--
DON'T WORRY, ANTHONY, I GOT IT!
WE'LL GO WITH THE FAT, PRETTY TOMCAT. MY HUSBAND WILL COME FETCH HIM RIGHT BEFORE CHRISTMAS.
ME? WHY ME?!
OUR TWO FRIENDS WILL LEARN TO GET USED TO ONE ANOTHER DURING THE TRIP.
OKAY, OKAY...
!
WE'LL TRY TO BECOME BUDDIES THEN, RIGHT, CUDDLES?

Travel, Travel

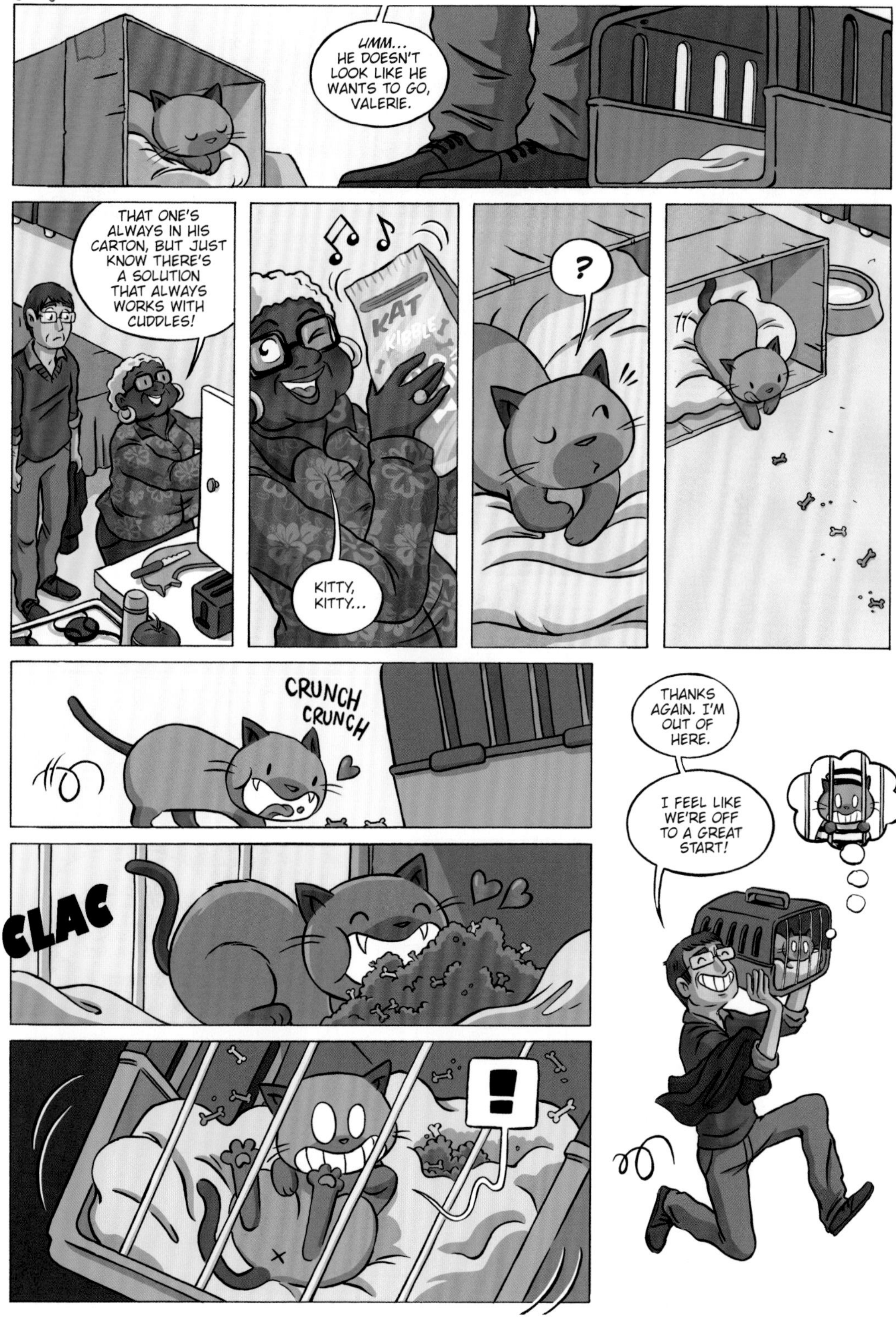
UMM... HE DOESN'T LOOK LIKE HE WANTS TO GO, VALERIE.
THAT ONE'S ALWAYS IN HIS CARTON, BUT JUST KNOW THERE'S A SOLUTION THAT ALWAYS WORKS WITH CUDDLES!
KAT KIBBLE
KITTY, KITTY...
?
CRUNCH CRUNCH
CLAC
!
THANKS AGAIN. I'M OUT OF HERE.
I FEEL LIKE WE'RE OFF TO A GREAT START!

With All Discretion

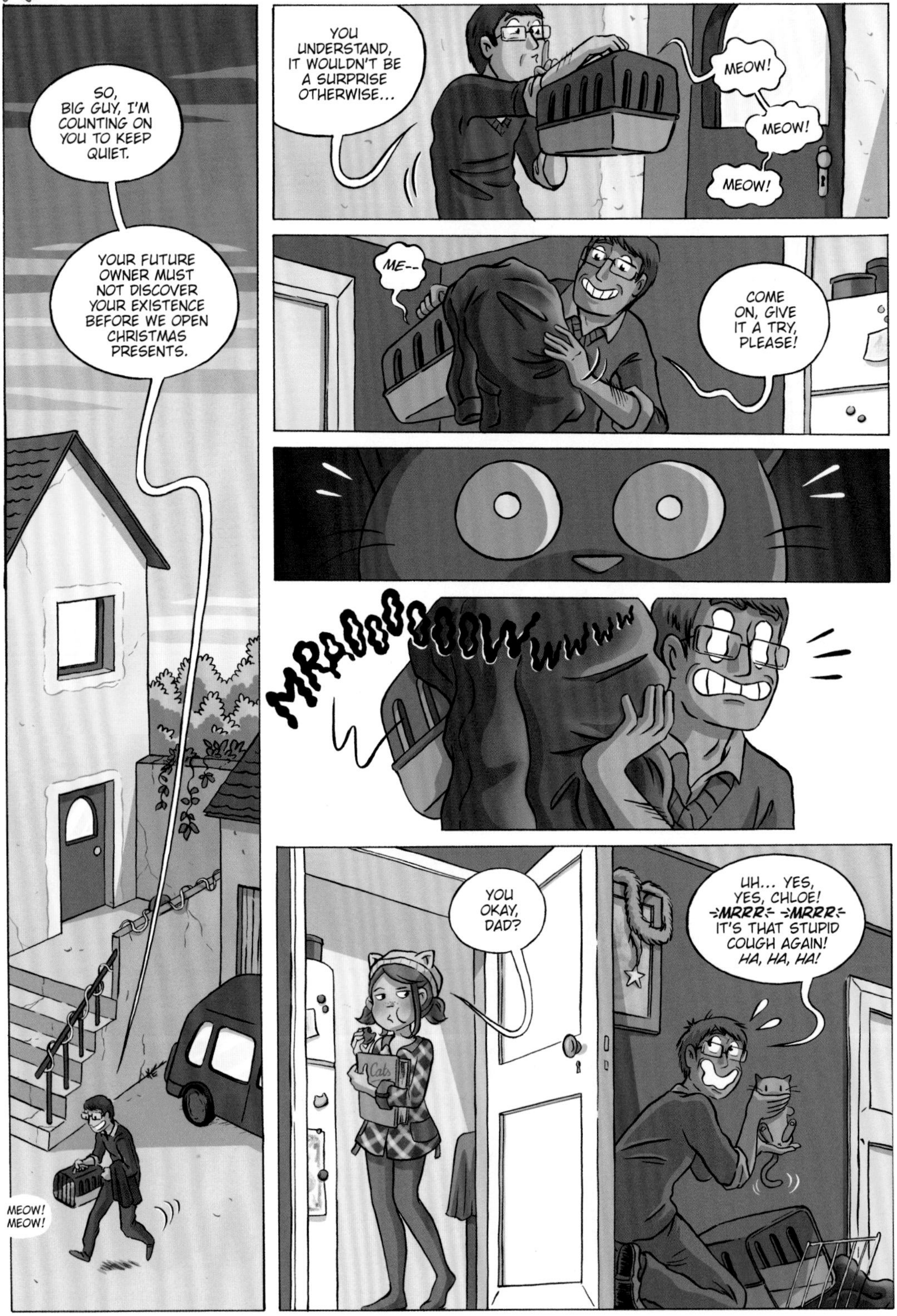

SO, BIG GUY, I'M COUNTING ON YOU TO KEEP QUIET.
YOUR FUTURE OWNER MUST NOT DISCOVER YOUR EXISTENCE BEFORE WE OPEN CHRISTMAS PRESENTS.
MEOW! MEOW!
YOU UNDERSTAND, IT WOULDN'T BE A SURPRISE OTHERWISE...
MEOW!
MEOW!
MEOW!
ME--
COME ON, GIVE IT A TRY, PLEASE!
MRAOOOOOOWWWWW
YOU OKAY, DAD?
UH... YES, YES, CHLOE! *MRRR* *MRRR* IT'S THAT STUPID COUGH AGAIN! HA, HA, HA!

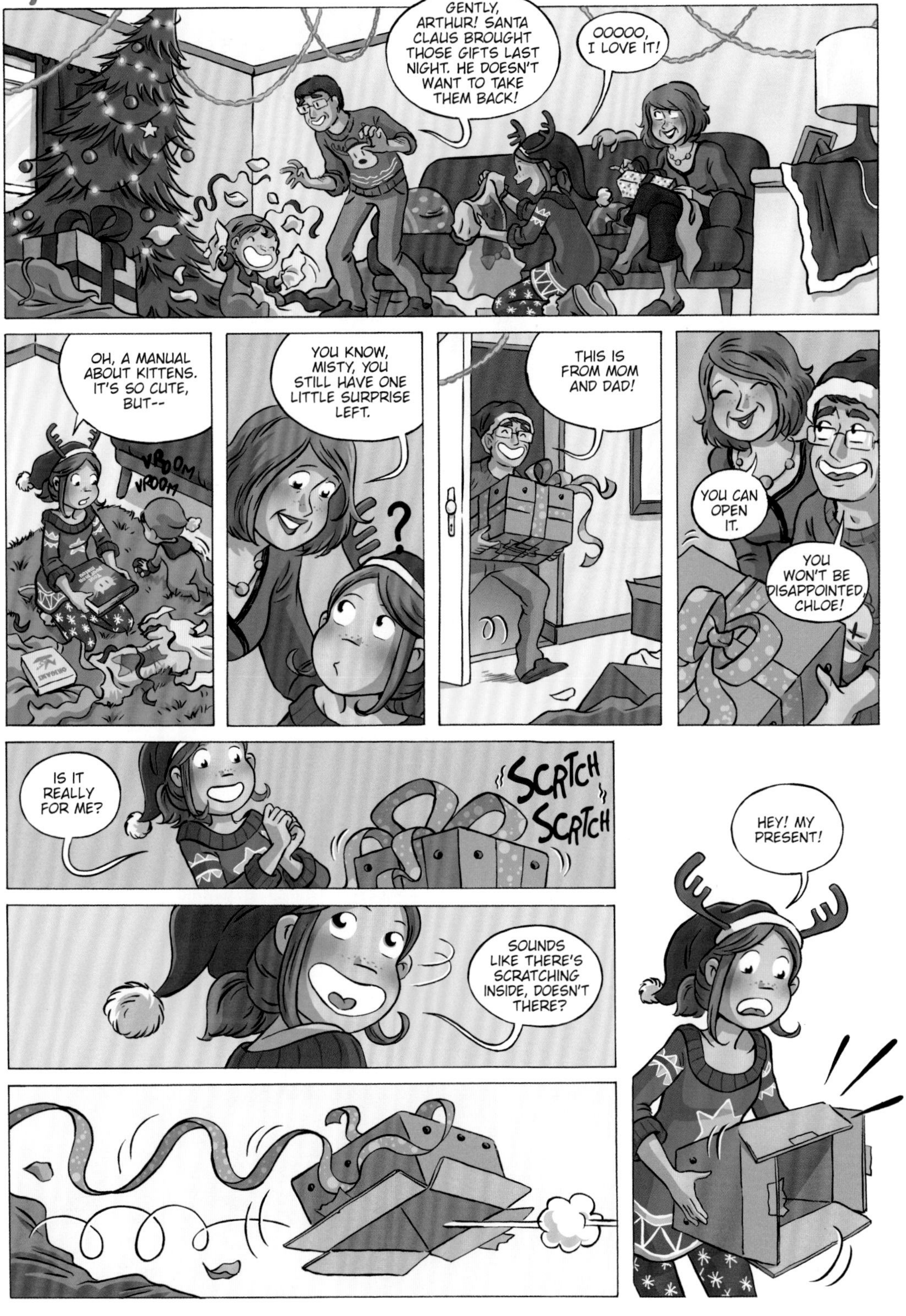
GENTLY, ARTHUR! SANTA CLAUS BROUGHT THOSE GIFTS LAST NIGHT. HE DOESN'T WANT TO TAKE THEM BACK!
OOOOO, I LOVE IT!
OH, A MANUAL ABOUT KITTENS. IT'S SO CUTE, BUT--
VROOM VROOM
YOU KNOW, MISTY, YOU STILL HAVE ONE LITTLE SURPRISE LEFT.
?
THIS IS FROM MOM AND DAD!
YOU CAN OPEN IT.
YOU WON'T BE DISAPPOINTED, CHLOE!
IS IT REALLY FOR ME?
SCRTCH SCRTCH
SOUNDS LIKE THERE'S SCRATCHING INSIDE, DOESN'T THERE?
HEY! MY PRESENT!

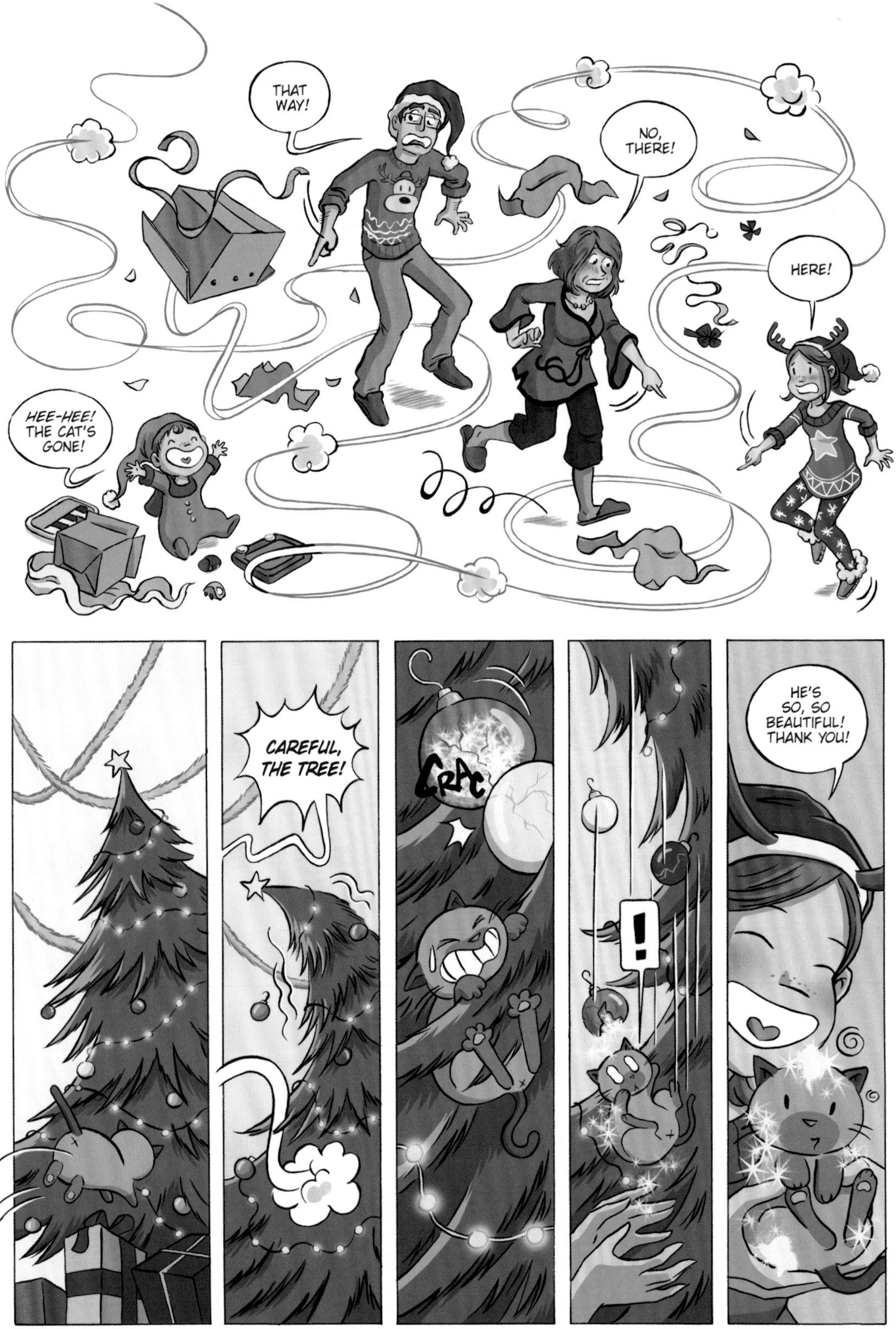
THAT WAY!
NO, THERE!
HERE!
HEE-HEE! THE CAT'S GONE!
CAREFUL, THE TREE!
CRAC
!
HE'S SO, SO BEAUTIFUL! THANK YOU!

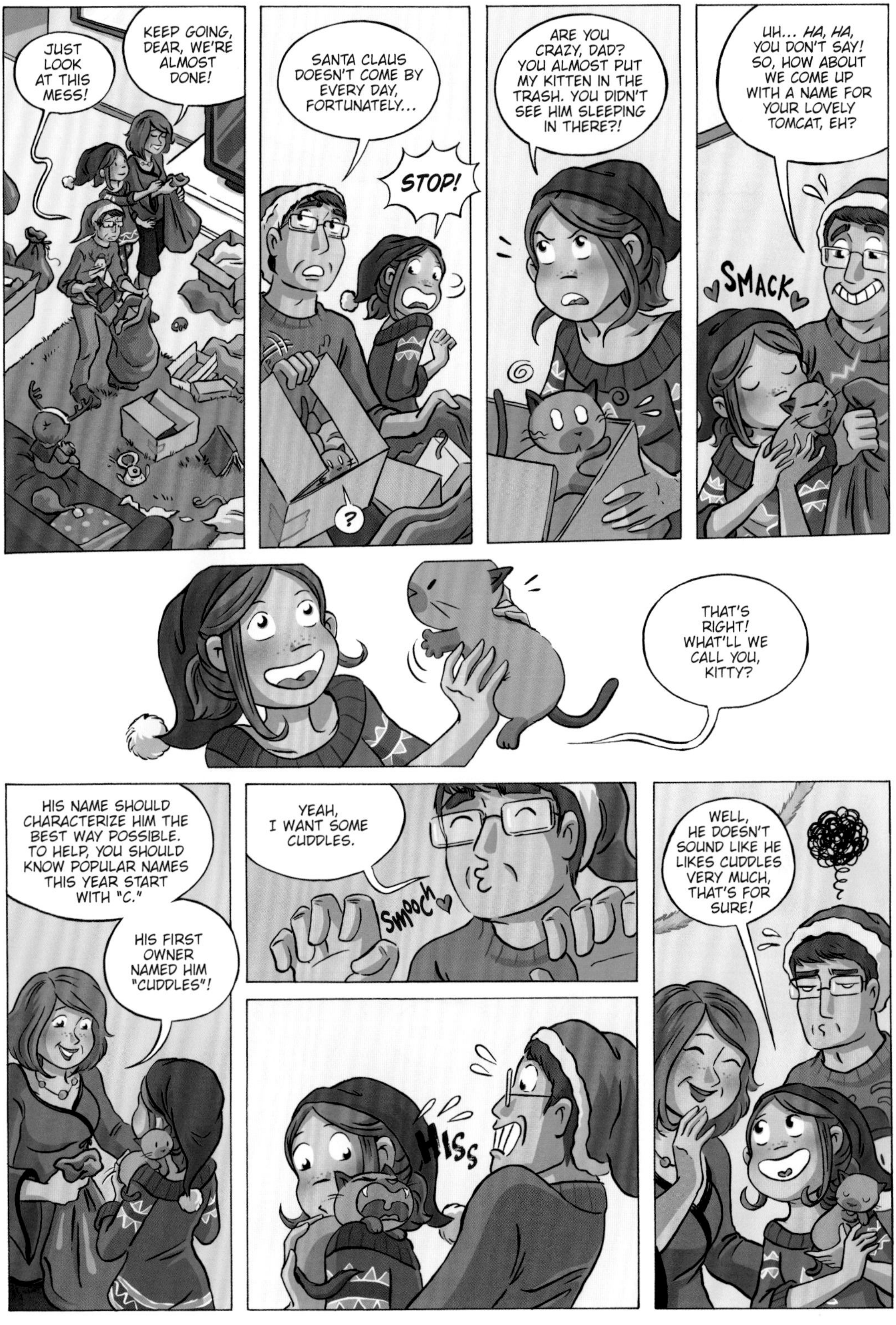
JUST LOOK AT THIS MESS!
KEEP GOING, DEAR, WE'RE ALMOST DONE!
SANTA CLAUS DOESN'T COME BY EVERY DAY, FORTUNATELY...
STOP!
?
ARE YOU CRAZY, DAD? YOU ALMOST PUT MY KITTEN IN THE TRASH. YOU DIDN'T SEE HIM SLEEPING IN THERE?!
UH... HA, HA, YOU DON'T SAY! SO, HOW ABOUT WE COME UP WITH A NAME FOR YOUR LOVELY TOMCAT, EH?
SMACK
THAT'S RIGHT! WHAT'LL WE CALL YOU, KITTY?
HIS NAME SHOULD CHARACTERIZE HIM THE BEST WAY POSSIBLE. TO HELP, YOU SHOULD KNOW POPULAR NAMES THIS YEAR START WITH "C."
HIS FIRST OWNER NAMED HIM "CUDDLES"!
YEAH, I WANT SOME CUDDLES.
SMOOCH
HISS
WELL, HE DOESN'T SOUND LIKE HE LIKES CUDDLES VERY MUCH, THAT'S FOR SURE!

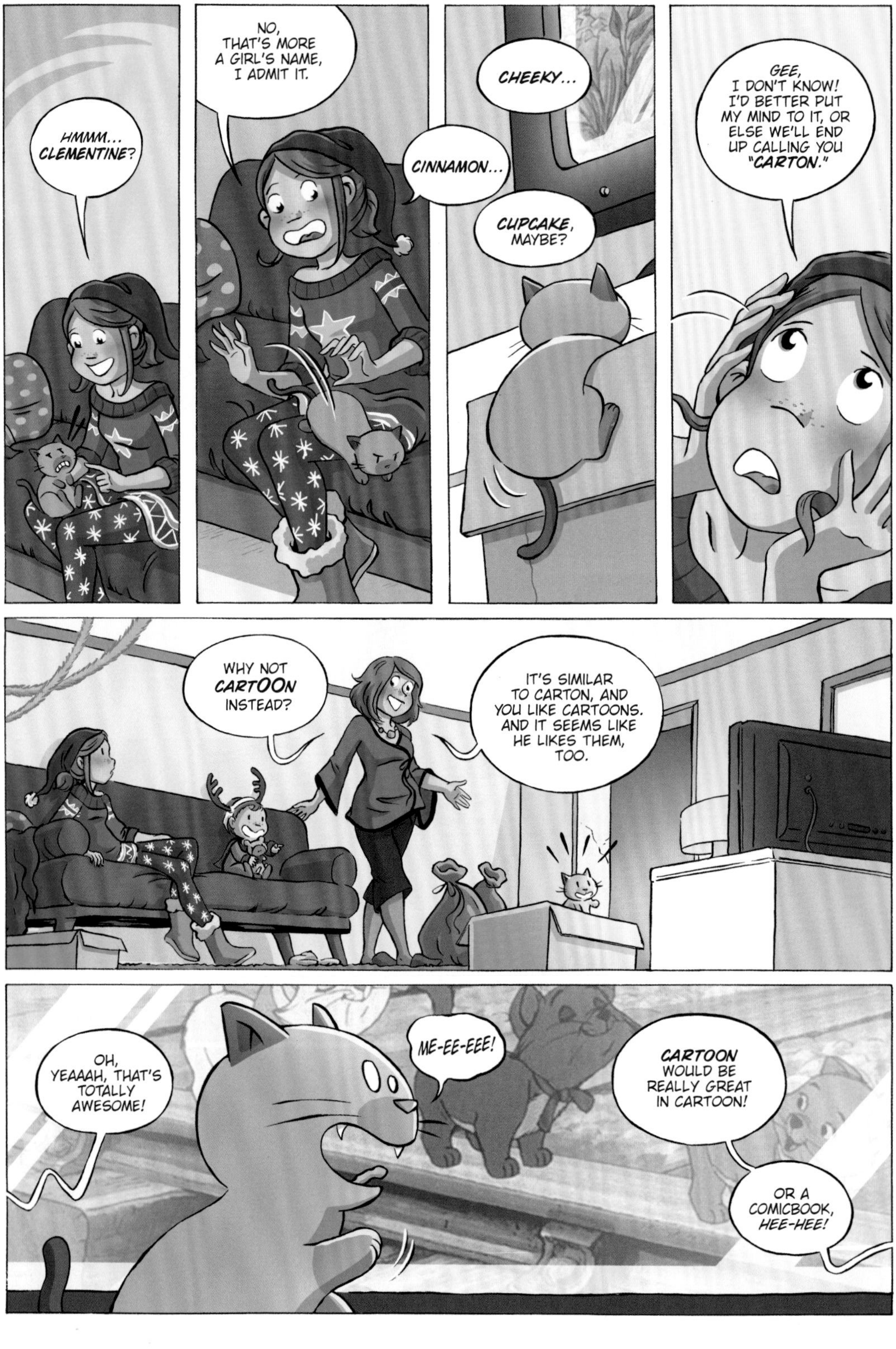
HMMM... CLEMENTINE?
NO, THAT'S MORE A GIRL'S NAME, I ADMIT IT.
CHEEKY...
CINNAMON...
CUPCAKE, MAYBE?
GEE, I DON'T KNOW! I'D BETTER PUT MY MIND TO IT, OR ELSE WE'LL END UP CALLING YOU "CARTON."
WHY NOT CARTOON INSTEAD?
IT'S SIMILAR TO CARTON, AND YOU LIKE CARTOONS. AND IT SEEMS LIKE HE LIKES THEM, TOO.
OH, YEAAAH, THAT'S TOTALLY AWESOME!
ME-EE-EEE!
CARTOON WOULD BE REALLY GREAT IN CARTOON!
OR A COMICBOOK, HEE-HEE!

Up The Creek Without A Paddle

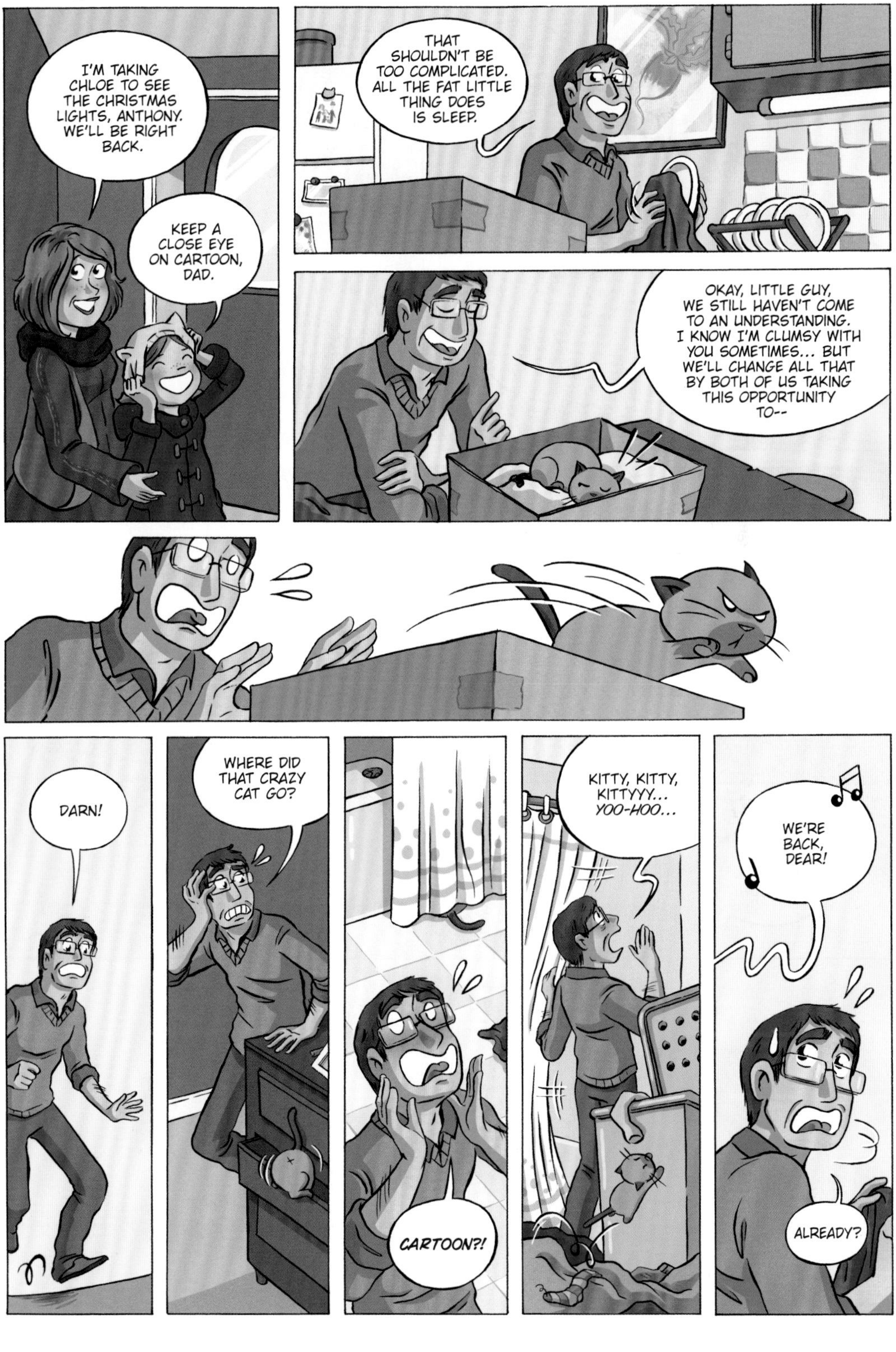
I'M TAKING CHLOE TO SEE THE CHRISTMAS LIGHTS, ANTHONY. WE'LL BE RIGHT BACK.
KEEP A CLOSE EYE ON CARTOON, DAD.
THAT SHOULDN'T BE TOO COMPLICATED. ALL THE FAT LITTLE THING DOES IS SLEEP.
OKAY, LITTLE GUY, WE STILL HAVEN'T COME TO AN UNDERSTANDING. I KNOW I'M CLUMSY WITH YOU SOMETIMES... BUT WE'LL CHANGE ALL THAT BY BOTH OF US TAKING THIS OPPORTUNITY TO--
DARN!
WHERE DID THAT CRAZY CAT GO?
CARTOON?!
KITTY, KITTY, KITTYYY... *YOO-HOO...*
WE'RE BACK, DEAR!
ALREADY?

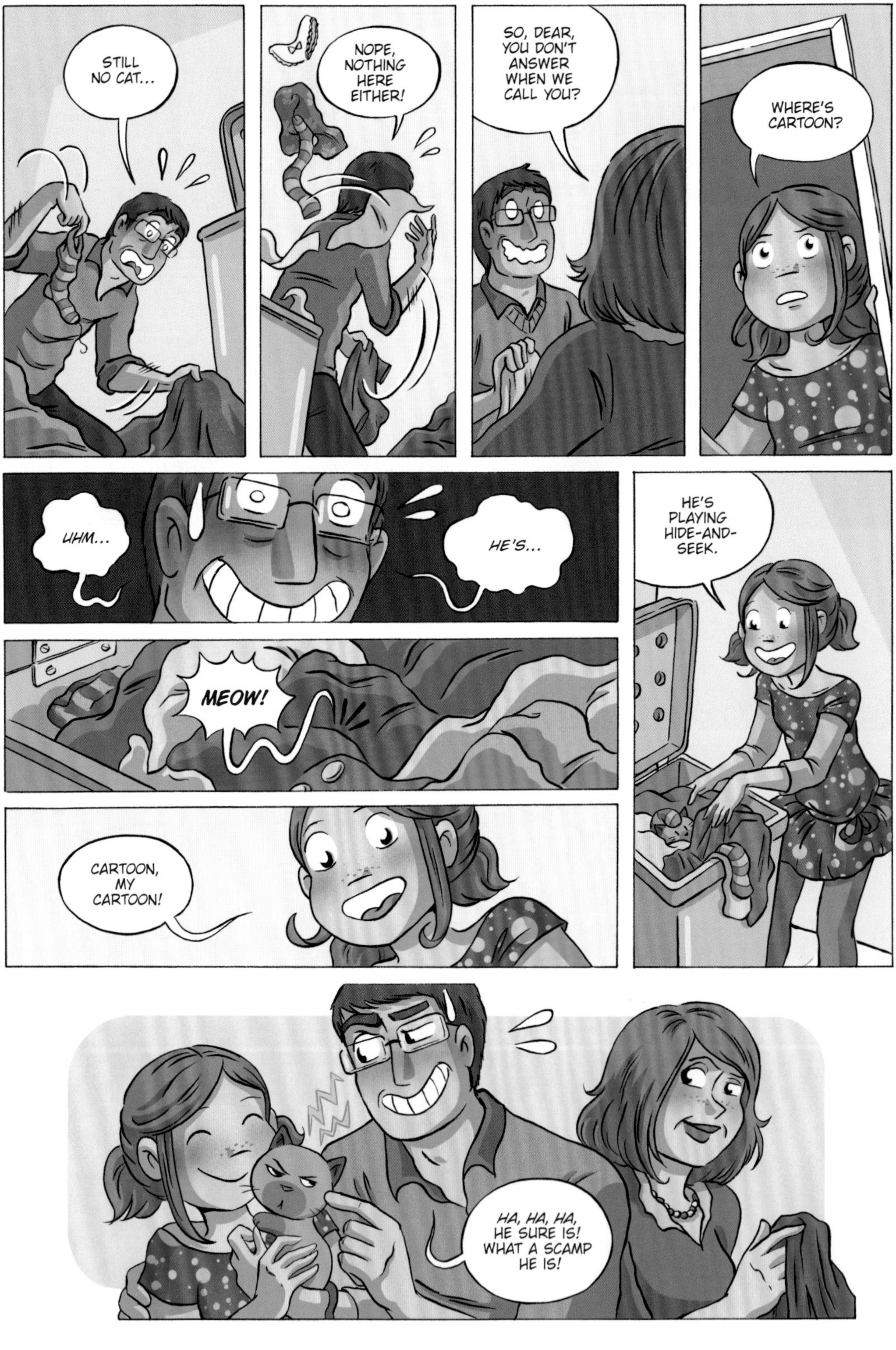
STILL NO CAT...
NOPE, NOTHING HERE EITHER!
SO, DEAR, YOU DON'T ANSWER WHEN WE CALL YOU?
WHERE'S CARTOON?
UHM...
HE'S...
HE'S PLAYING HIDE-AND-SEEK.
MEOW!
CARTOON, MY CARTOON!
HA, HA, HA, HE SURE IS! WHAT A SCAMP HE IS!

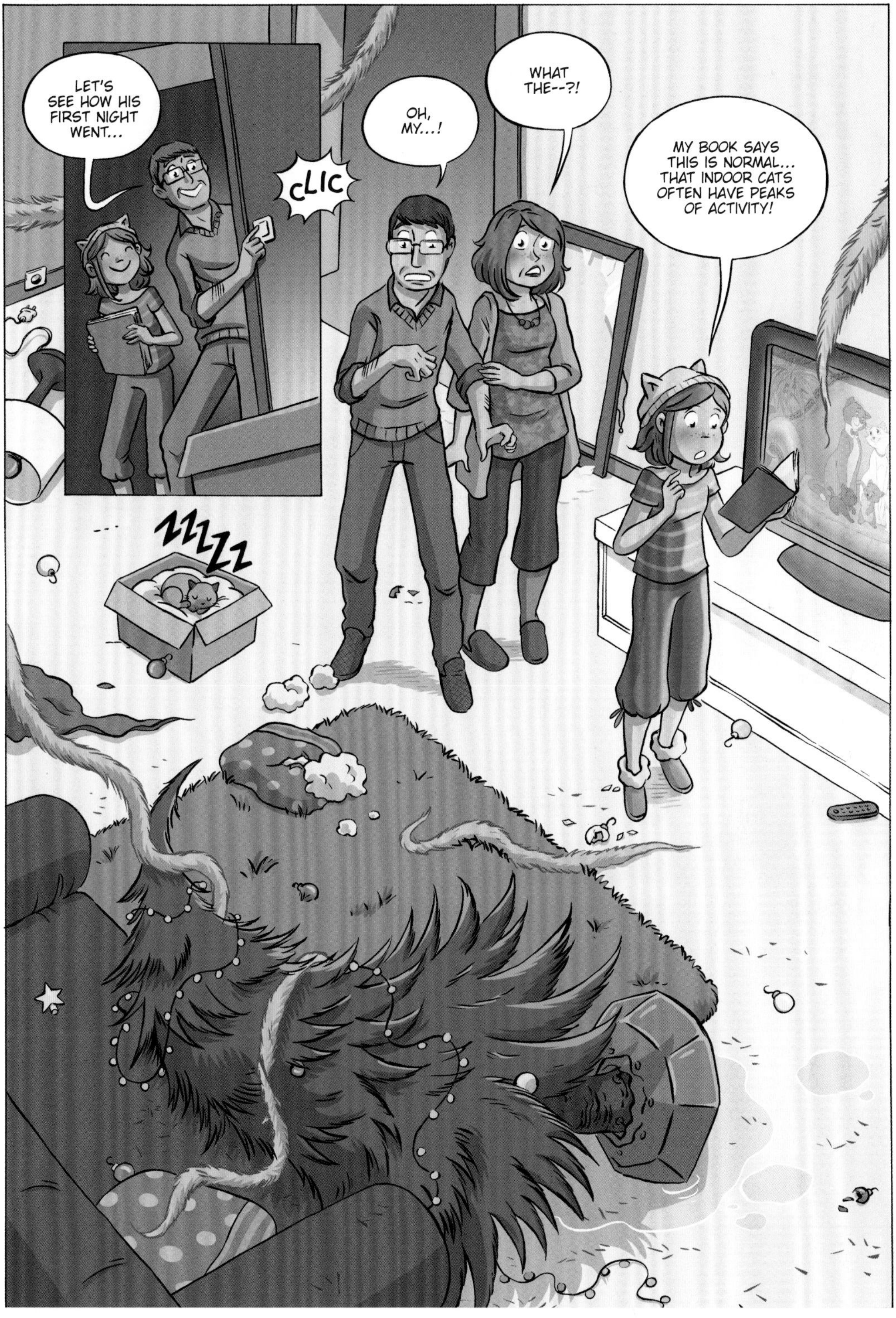
LET'S SEE HOW HIS FIRST NIGHT WENT...
CLIC
OH, MY...!
WHAT THE--?!
MY BOOK SAYS THIS IS NORMAL... THAT INDOOR CATS OFTEN HAVE PEAKS OF ACTIVITY!
ZZZZZ

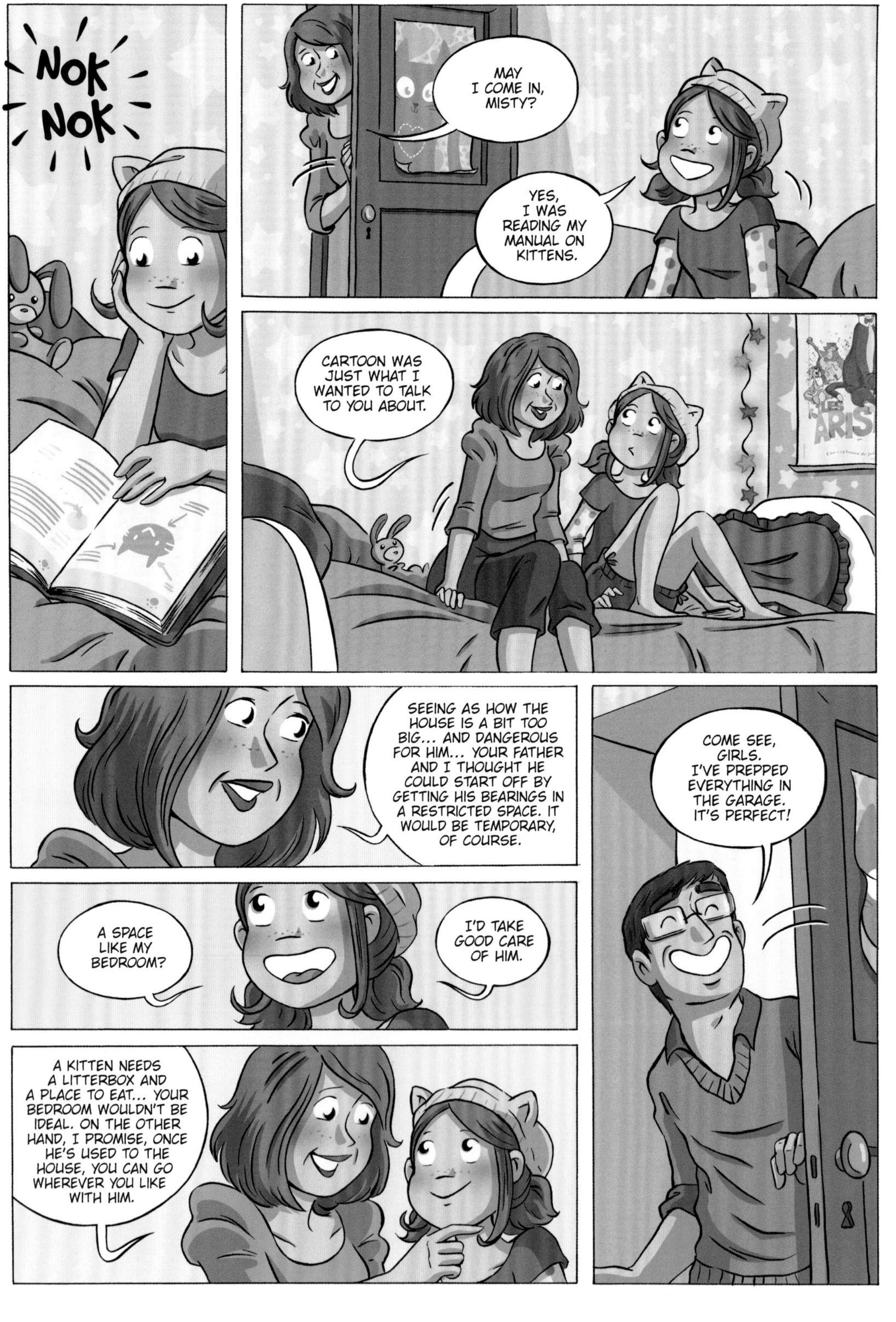
NOK NOK
MAY I COME IN, MISTY?
YES, I WAS READING MY MANUAL ON KITTENS.
CARTOON WAS JUST WHAT I WANTED TO TALK TO YOU ABOUT.
SEEING AS HOW THE HOUSE IS A BIT TOO BIG... AND DANGEROUS FOR HIM... YOUR FATHER AND I THOUGHT HE COULD START OFF BY GETTING HIS BEARINGS IN A RESTRICTED SPACE. IT WOULD BE TEMPORARY, OF COURSE.
A SPACE LIKE MY BEDROOM?
I'D TAKE GOOD CARE OF HIM.
A KITTEN NEEDS A LITTERBOX AND A PLACE TO EAT... YOUR BEDROOM WOULDN'T BE IDEAL. ON THE OTHER HAND, I PROMISE, ONCE HE'S USED TO THE HOUSE, YOU CAN GO WHEREVER YOU LIKE WITH HIM.
COME SEE, GIRLS. I'VE PREPPED EVERYTHING IN THE GARAGE. IT'S PERFECT!

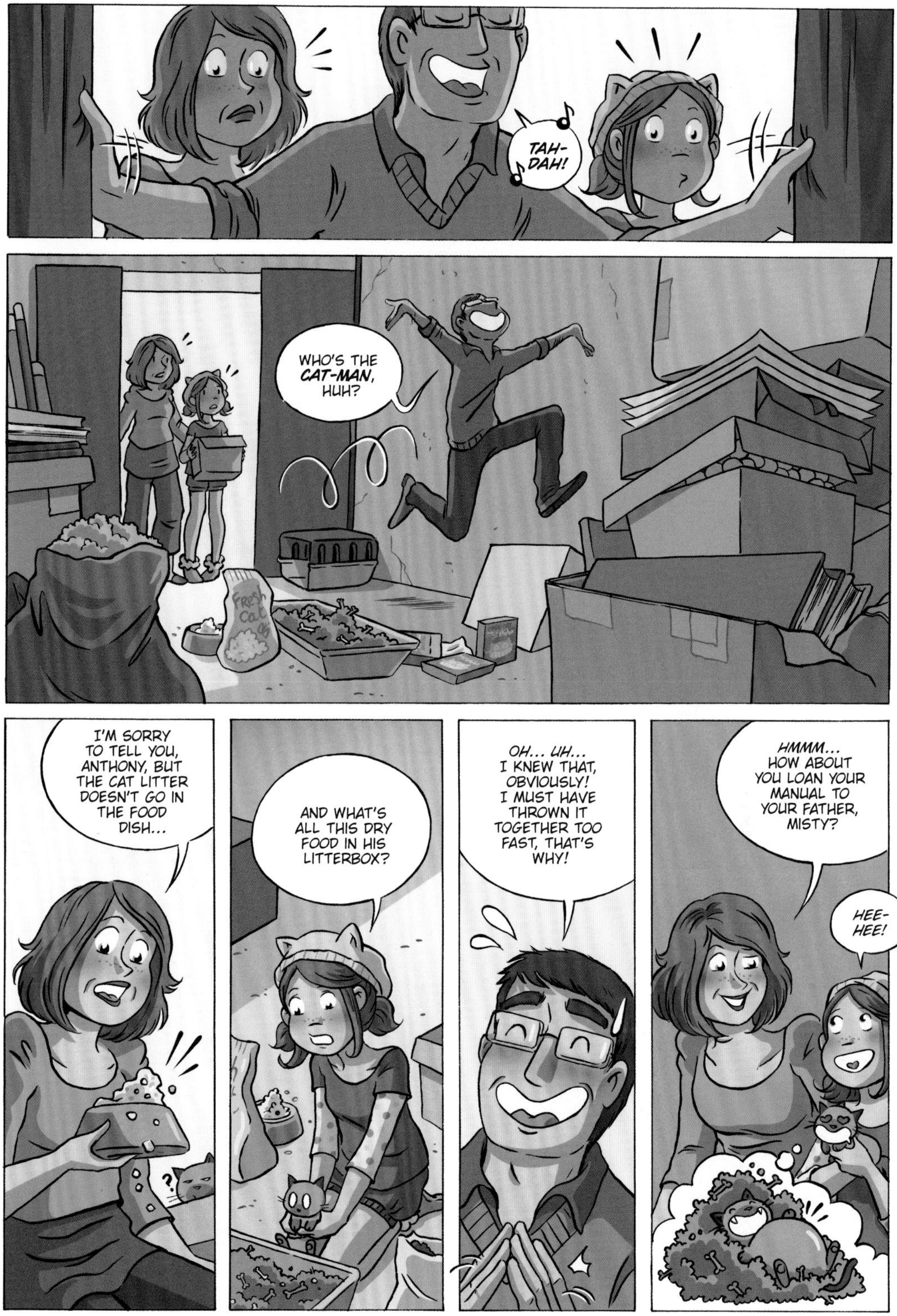
TAH-DAH!
WHO'S THE CAT-MAN, HUH?
Fresh Cat
I'M SORRY TO TELL YOU, ANTHONY, BUT THE CAT LITTER DOESN'T GO IN THE FOOD DISH...
AND WHAT'S ALL THIS DRY FOOD IN HIS LITTERBOX?
OH... UH... I KNEW THAT, OBVIOUSLY! I MUST HAVE THROWN IT TOGETHER TOO FAST, THAT'S WHY!
HMMM... HOW ABOUT YOU LOAN YOUR MANUAL TO YOUR FATHER, MISTY?
HEE-HEE!

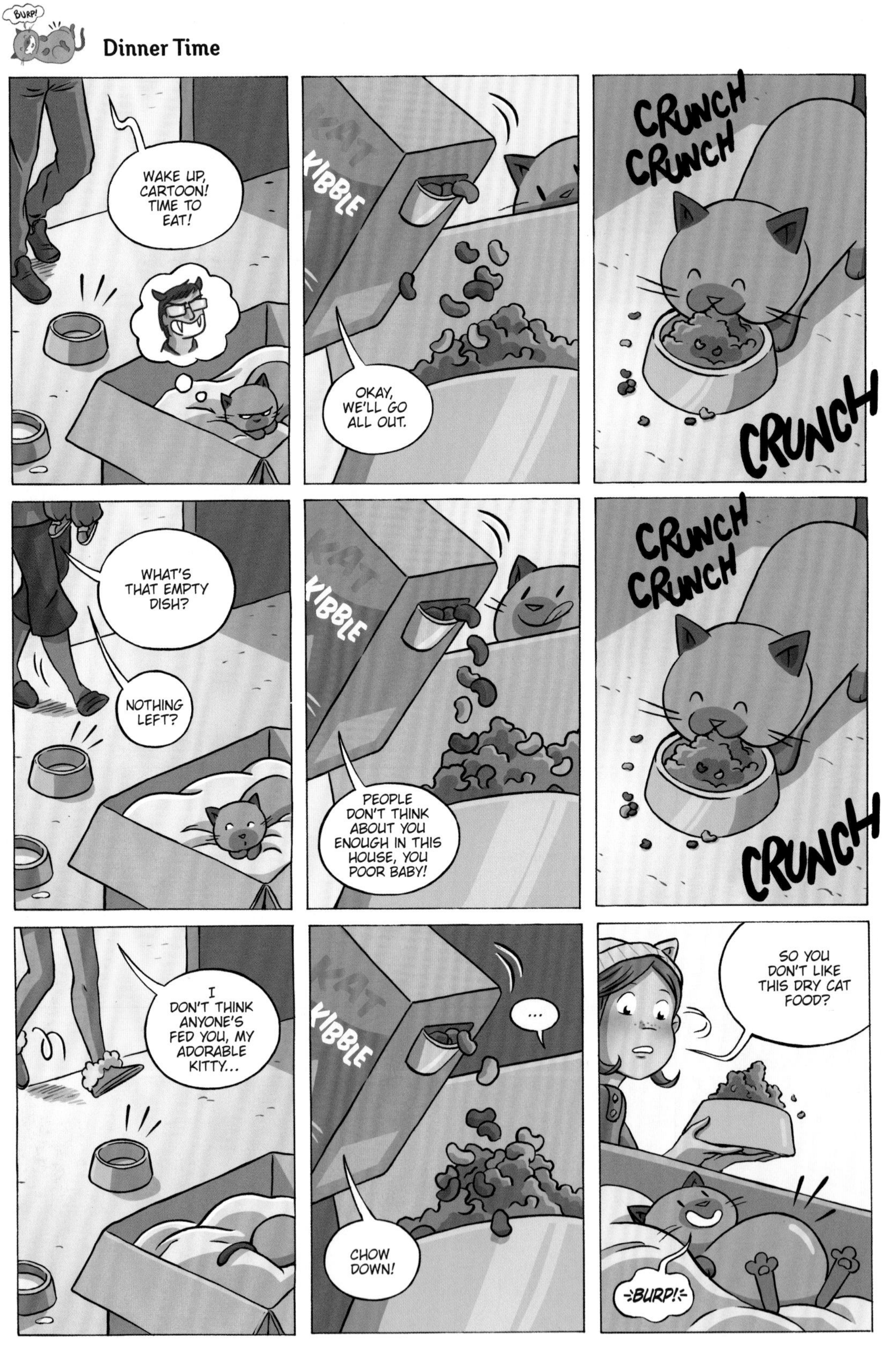
BURP!
WAKE UP, CARTOON! TIME TO EAT!
KAT KIBBLE
OKAY, WE'LL GO ALL OUT.
CRUNCH
CRUNCH
CRUNCH
WHAT'S THAT EMPTY DISH?
NOTHING LEFT?
KAT KIBBLE
PEOPLE DON'T THINK ABOUT YOU ENOUGH IN THIS HOUSE, YOU POOR BABY!
CRUNCH
CRUNCH
CRUNCH
I DON'T THINK ANYONE'S FED YOU, MY ADORABLE KITTY...
KAT KIBBLE
...
CHOW DOWN!
SO YOU DON'T LIKE THIS DRY CAT FOOD?
BURP!

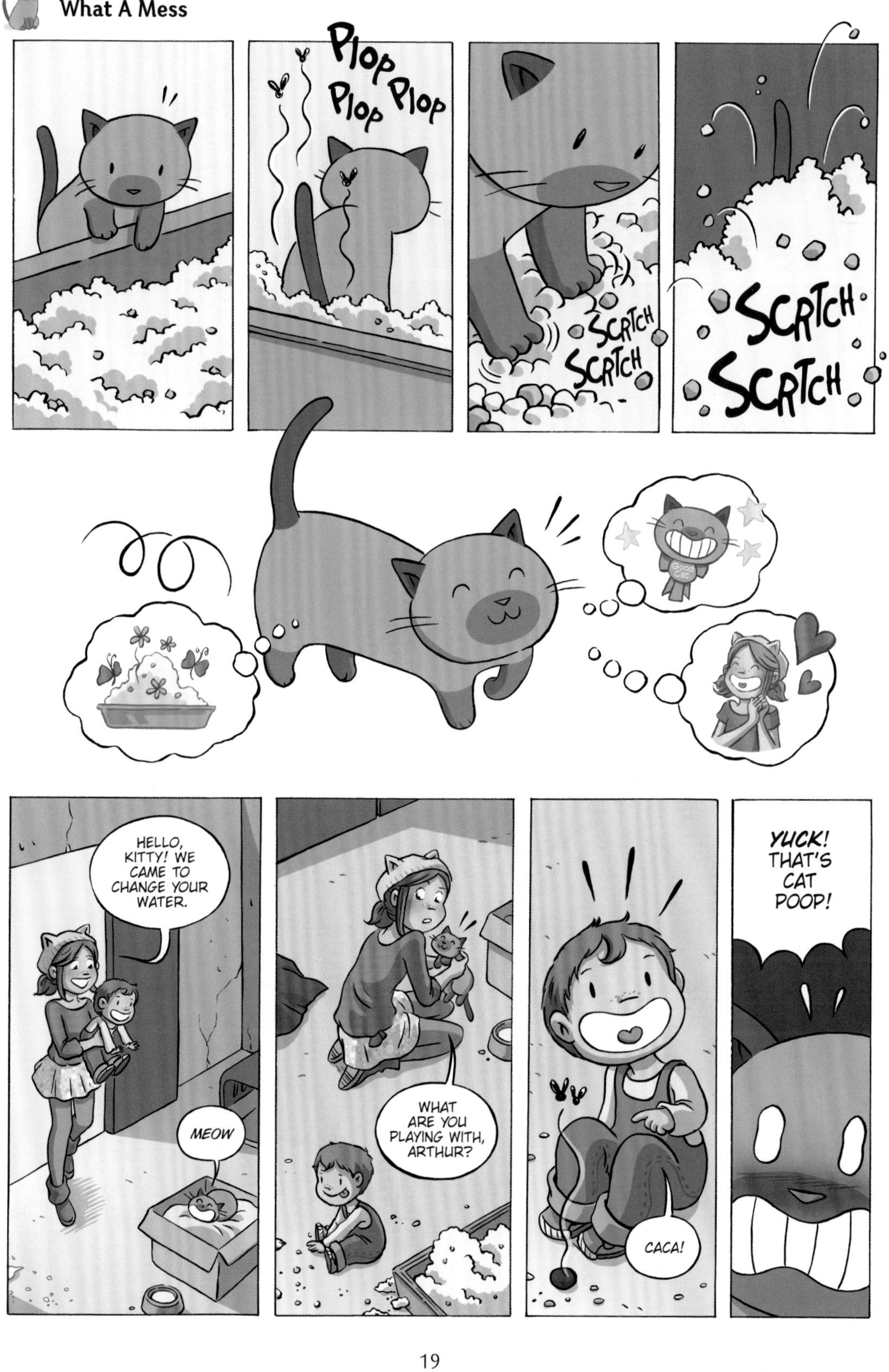
PLOP PLOP
PLOP PLOP
SCRTCH
SCRTCH
SCRTCH
SCRTCH
Good Cat
HELLO, KITTY! WE CAME TO CHANGE YOUR WATER.
MEOW
WHAT ARE YOU PLAYING WITH, ARTHUR?
CACA!
YUCK! THAT'S CAT POOP!

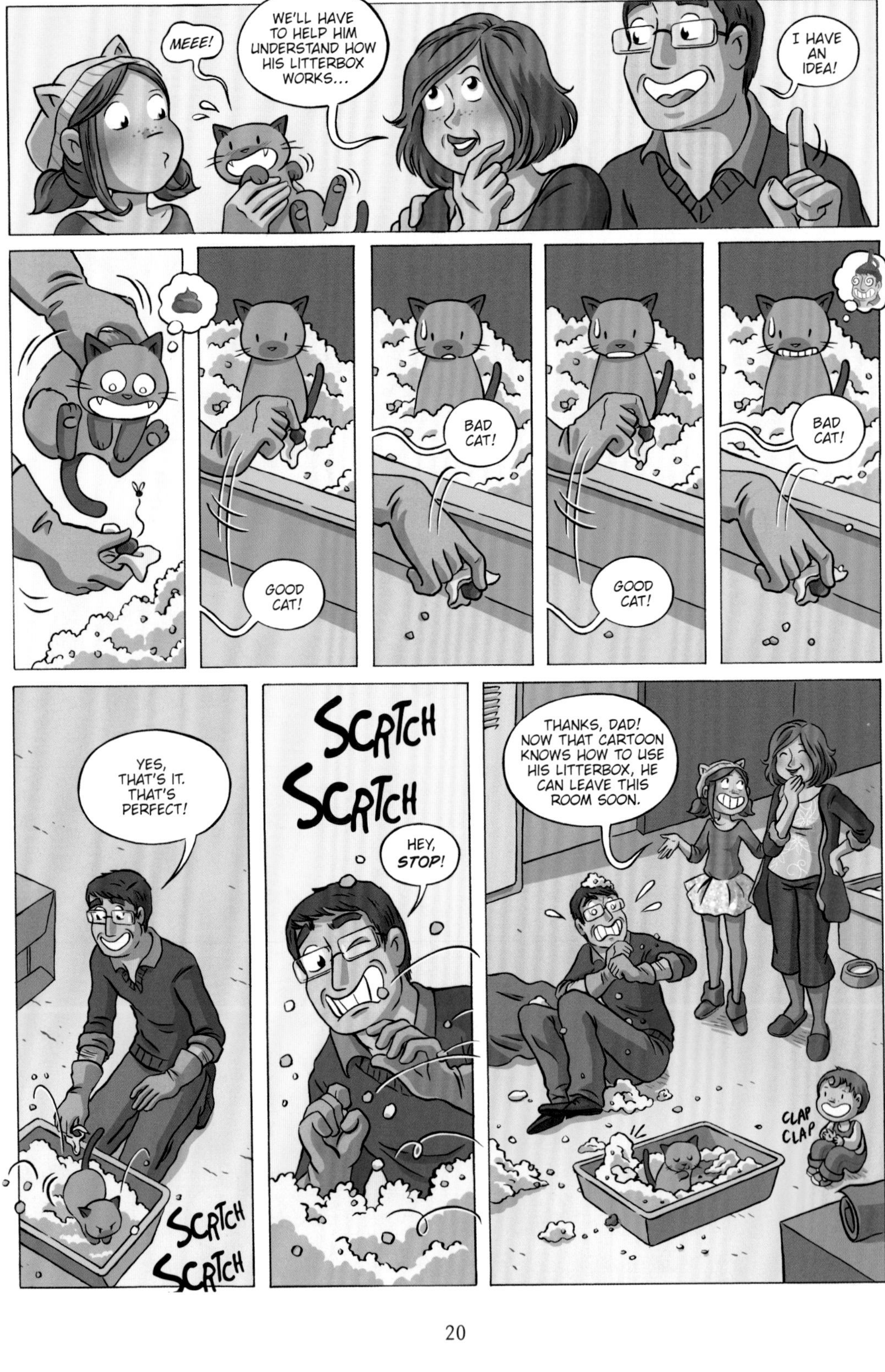
MEEE!
WE'LL HAVE TO HELP HIM UNDERSTAND HOW HIS LITTERBOX WORKS...
I HAVE AN IDEA!
GOOD CAT!
BAD CAT!
GOOD CAT!
BAD CAT!
YES, THAT'S IT. THAT'S PERFECT!
SCRTCH
SCRTCH
SCRTCH
SCRTCH
HEY, STOP!
THANKS, DAD! NOW THAT CARTOON KNOWS HOW TO USE HIS LITTERBOX, HE CAN LEAVE THIS ROOM SOON.
CLAP CLAP

A Laid-Back Attitude

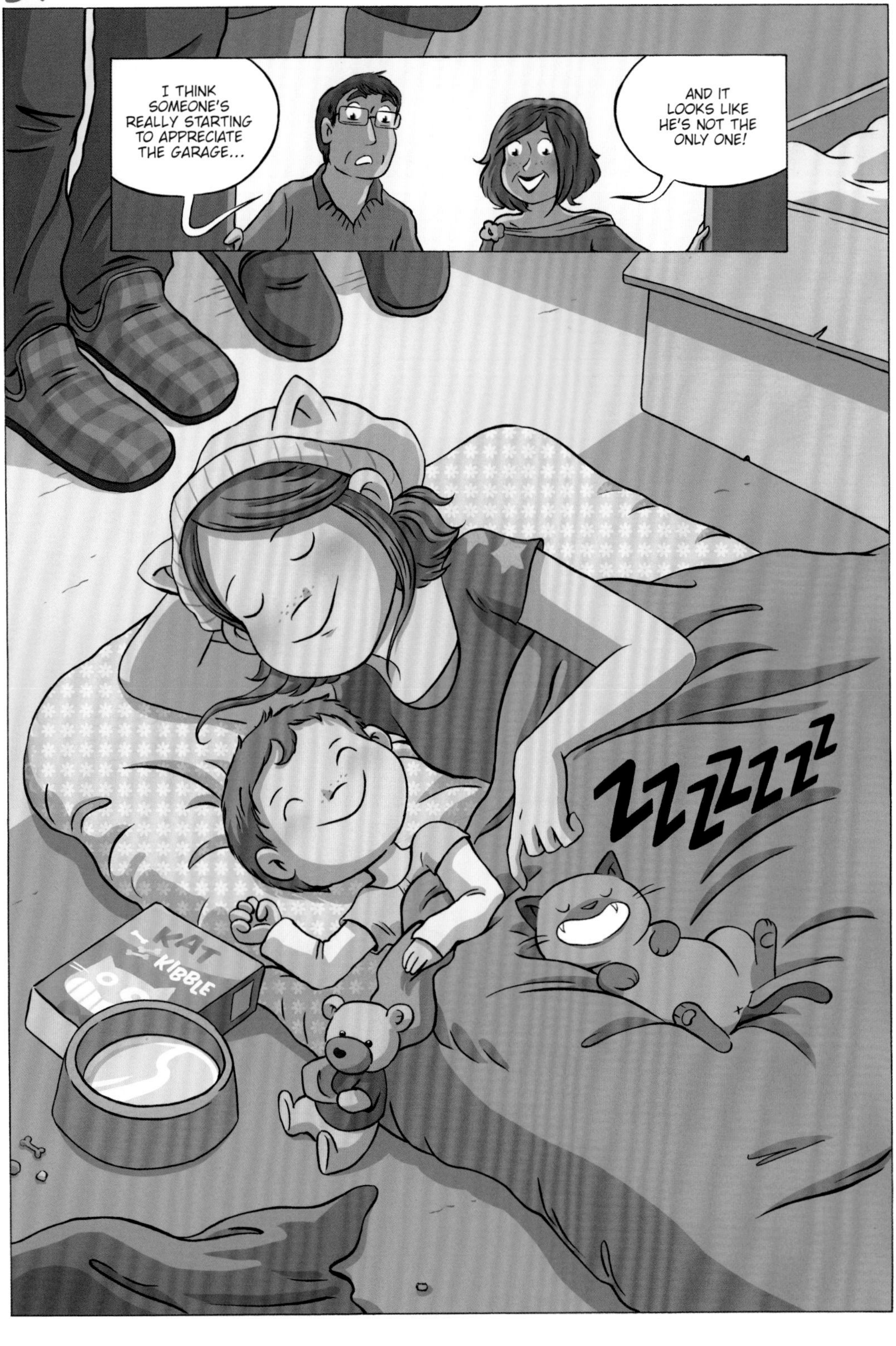
I THINK SOMEONE'S REALLY STARTING TO APPRECIATE THE GARAGE...
AND IT LOOKS LIKE HE'S NOT THE ONLY ONE!
ZZZZZZZ
KAT KIBBLE

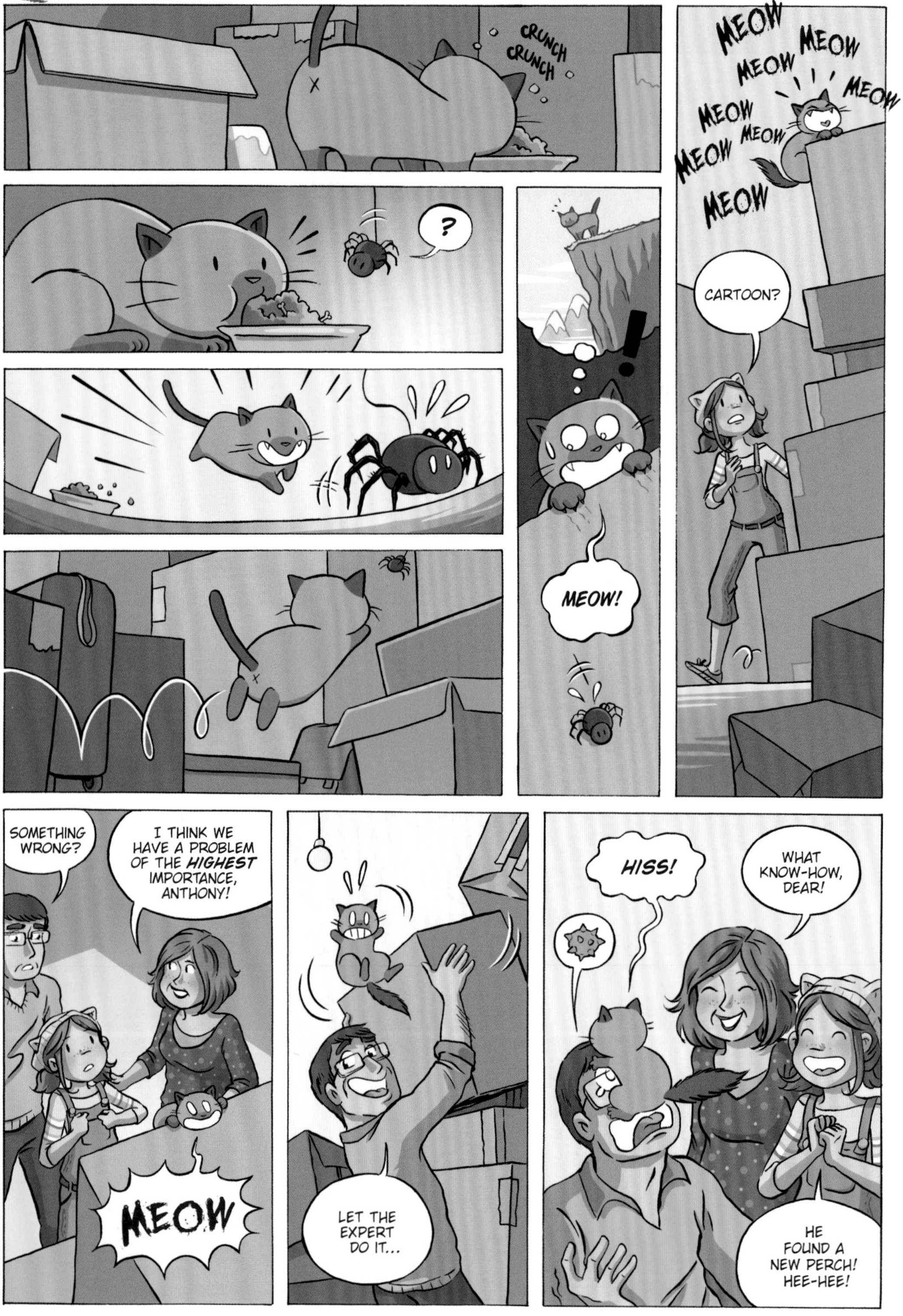
CRUNCH
CRUNCH
?
!
MEOW!
MEOW
MEOW
MEOW
MEOW
MEOW
MEOW
MEOW
MEOW
MEOW
CARTOON?
SOMETHING WRONG?
I THINK WE HAVE A PROBLEM OF THE ***HIGHEST*** IMPORTANCE, ANTHONY!
MEOW
LET THE EXPERT DO IT...
HISS!
WHAT KNOW-HOW, DEAR!
HE FOUND A NEW PERCH! HEE-HEE!

All Bets Are Off

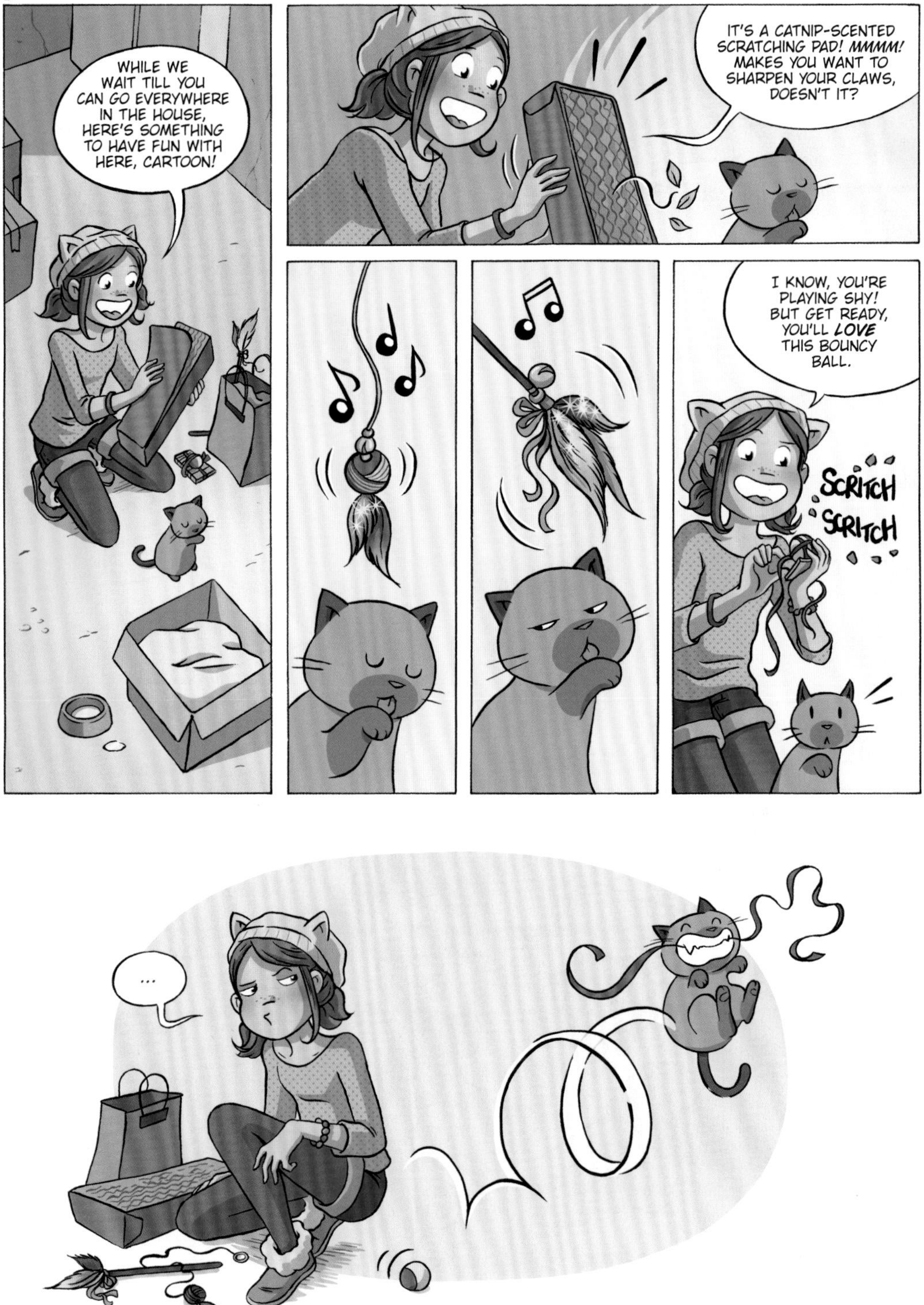

WHILE WE WAIT TILL YOU CAN GO EVERYWHERE IN THE HOUSE, HERE'S SOMETHING TO HAVE FUN WITH HERE, CARTOON!
IT'S A CATNIP-SCENTED SCRATCHING PAD! MMMM! MAKES YOU WANT TO SHARPEN YOUR CLAWS, DOESN'T IT?
I KNOW, YOU'RE PLAYING SHY! BUT GET READY, YOU'LL LOVE THIS BOUNCY BALL.
SCRITCH
SCRITCH
...

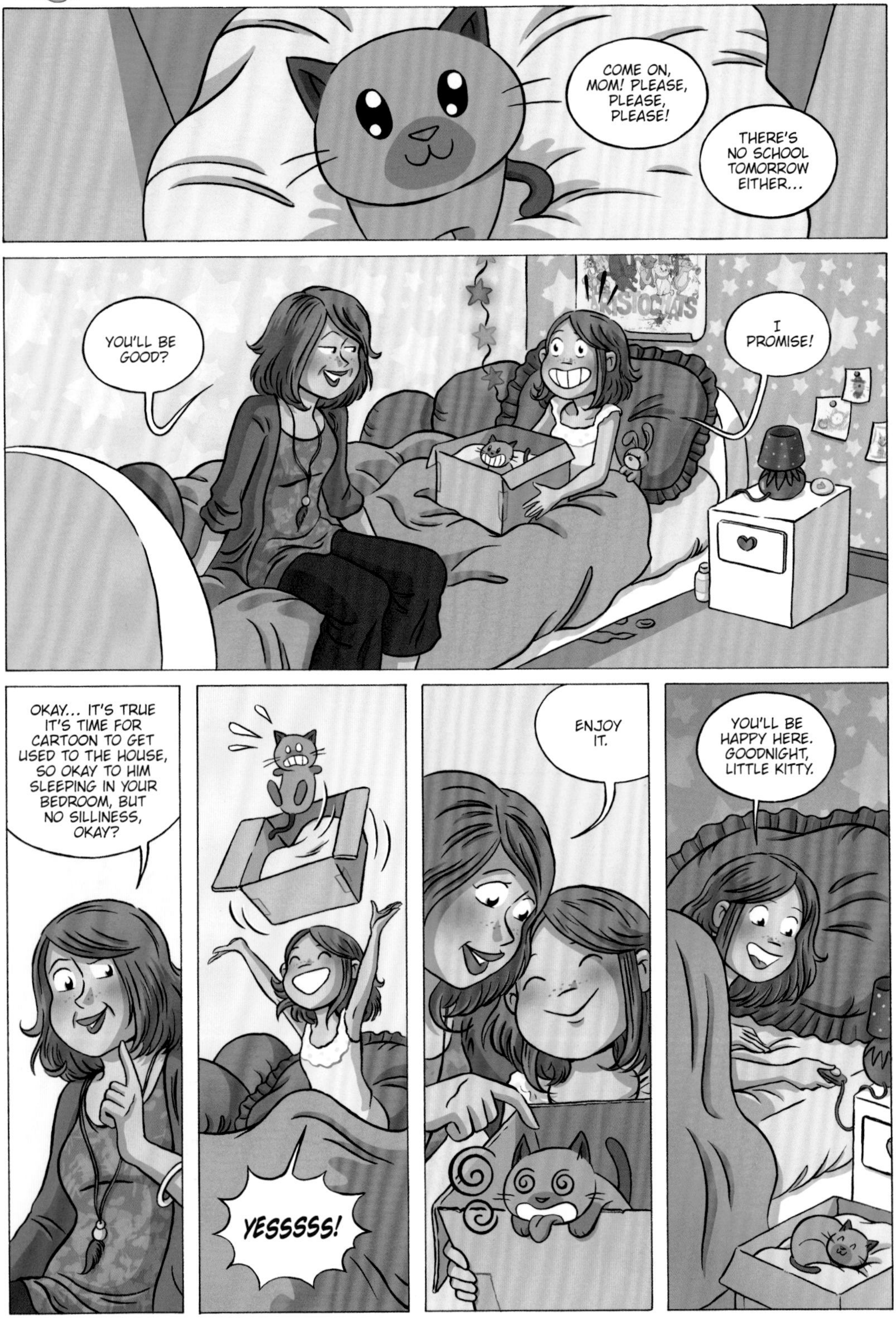
COME ON, MOM! PLEASE, PLEASE, PLEASE!
THERE'S NO SCHOOL TOMORROW EITHER...
YOU'LL BE GOOD?
I PROMISE!
OKAY... IT'S TRUE IT'S TIME FOR CARTOON TO GET USED TO THE HOUSE, SO OKAY TO HIM SLEEPING IN YOUR BEDROOM, BUT NO SILLINESS, OKAY?
YESSSSS!
ENJOY IT.
YOU'LL BE HAPPY HERE. GOODNIGHT, LITTLE KITTY.

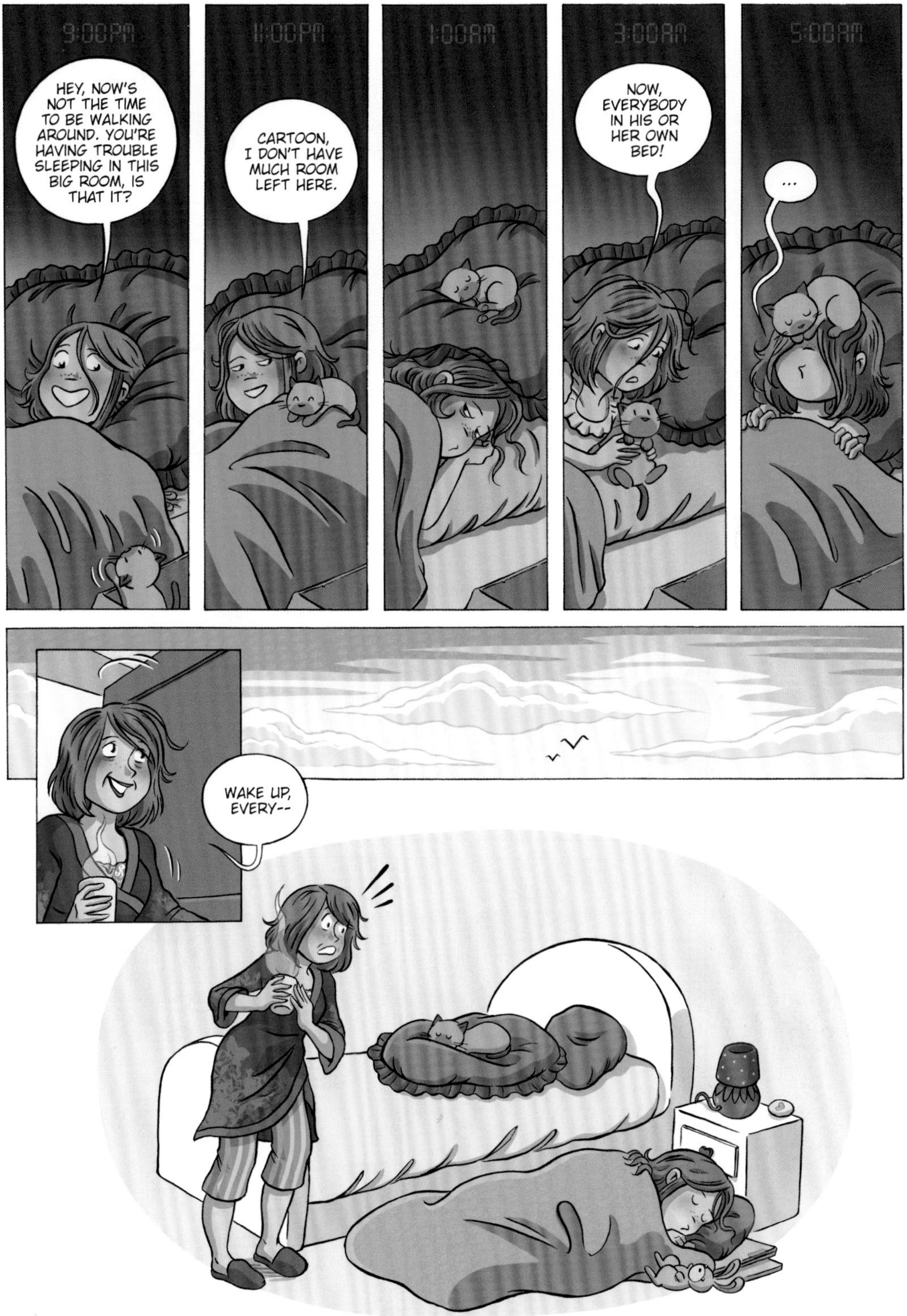
9:00PM
HEY, NOW'S NOT THE TIME TO BE WALKING AROUND. YOU'RE HAVING TROUBLE SLEEPING IN THIS BIG ROOM, IS THAT IT?
11:00PM
CARTOON, I DON'T HAVE MUCH ROOM LEFT HERE.
1:00AM
3:00AM
NOW, EVERYBODY IN HIS OR HER OWN BED!
5:00AM
...
WAKE UP, EVERY--

Bubble, Bubble...

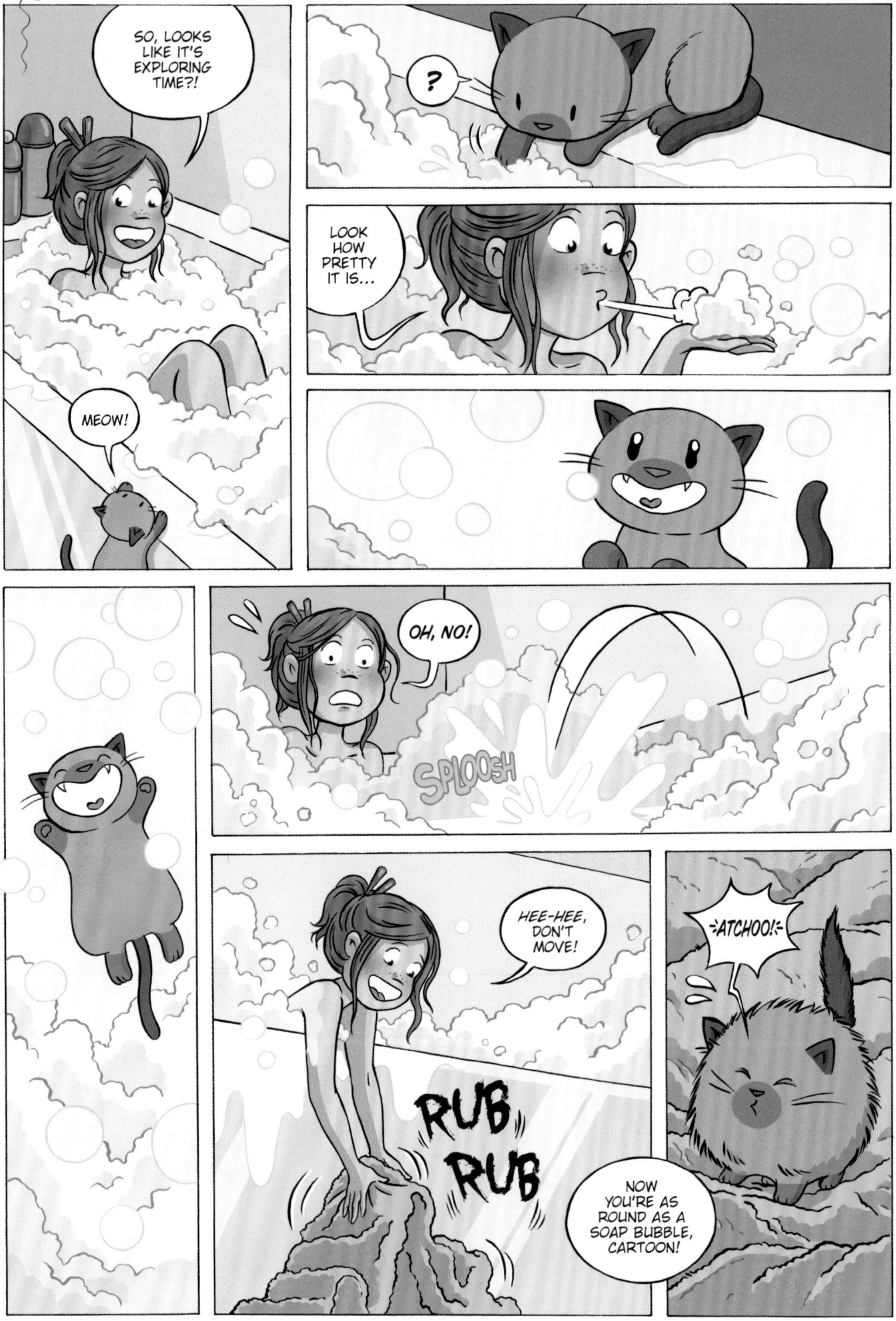

SO, LOOKS LIKE IT'S EXPLORING TIME?!
MEOW!
?
LOOK HOW PRETTY IT IS...
OH, NO!
SPLOOSH
HEE-HEE, DON'T MOVE!
RUB RUB
ATCHOO!
NOW YOU'RE AS ROUND AS A SOAP BUBBLE, CARTOON!

No Fear

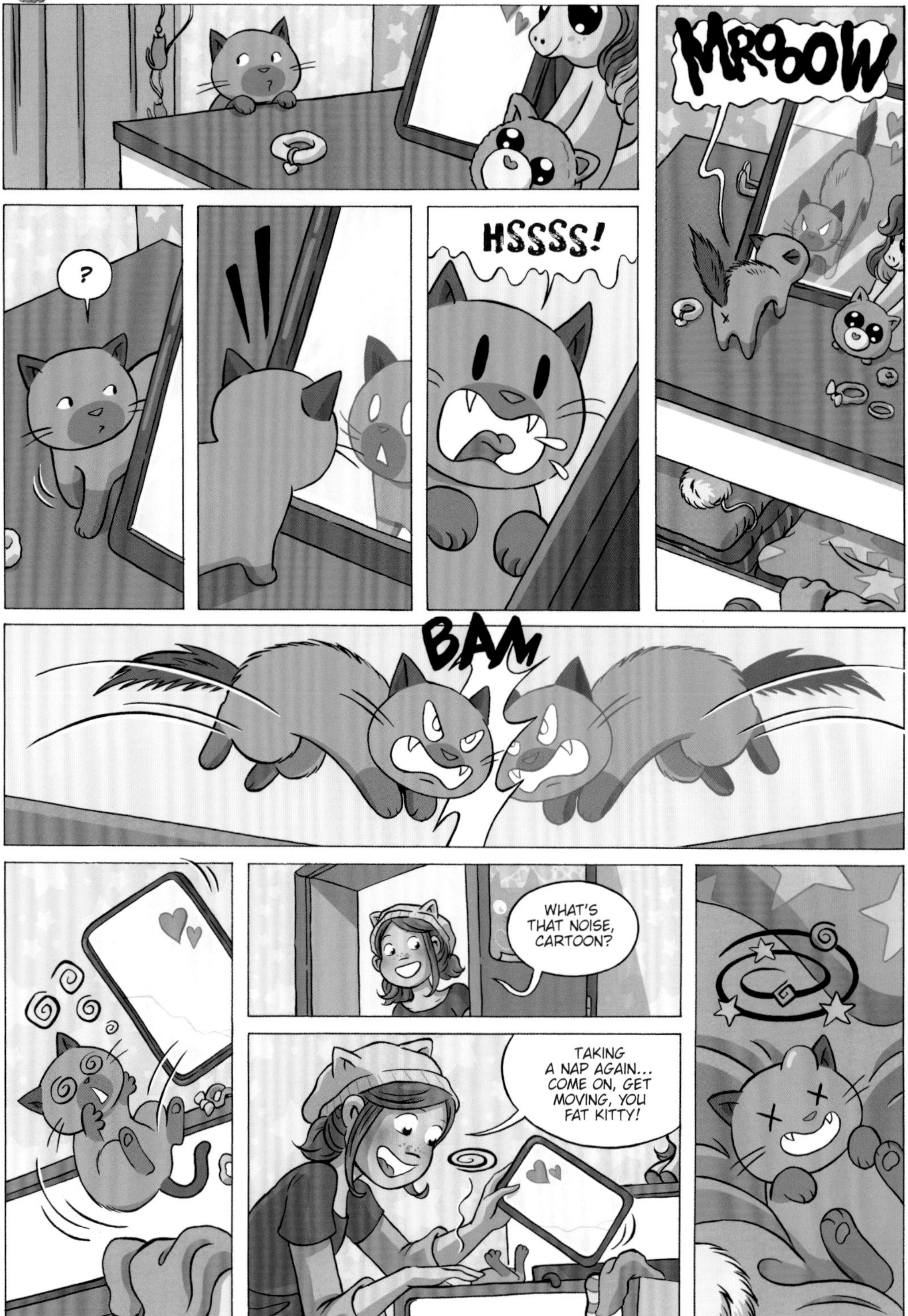

MROOOW
?
HSSSS!
BAM
WHAT'S THAT NOISE, CARTOON?
TAKING A NAP AGAIN... COME ON, GET MOVING, YOU FAT KITTY!

Dream Or Reality

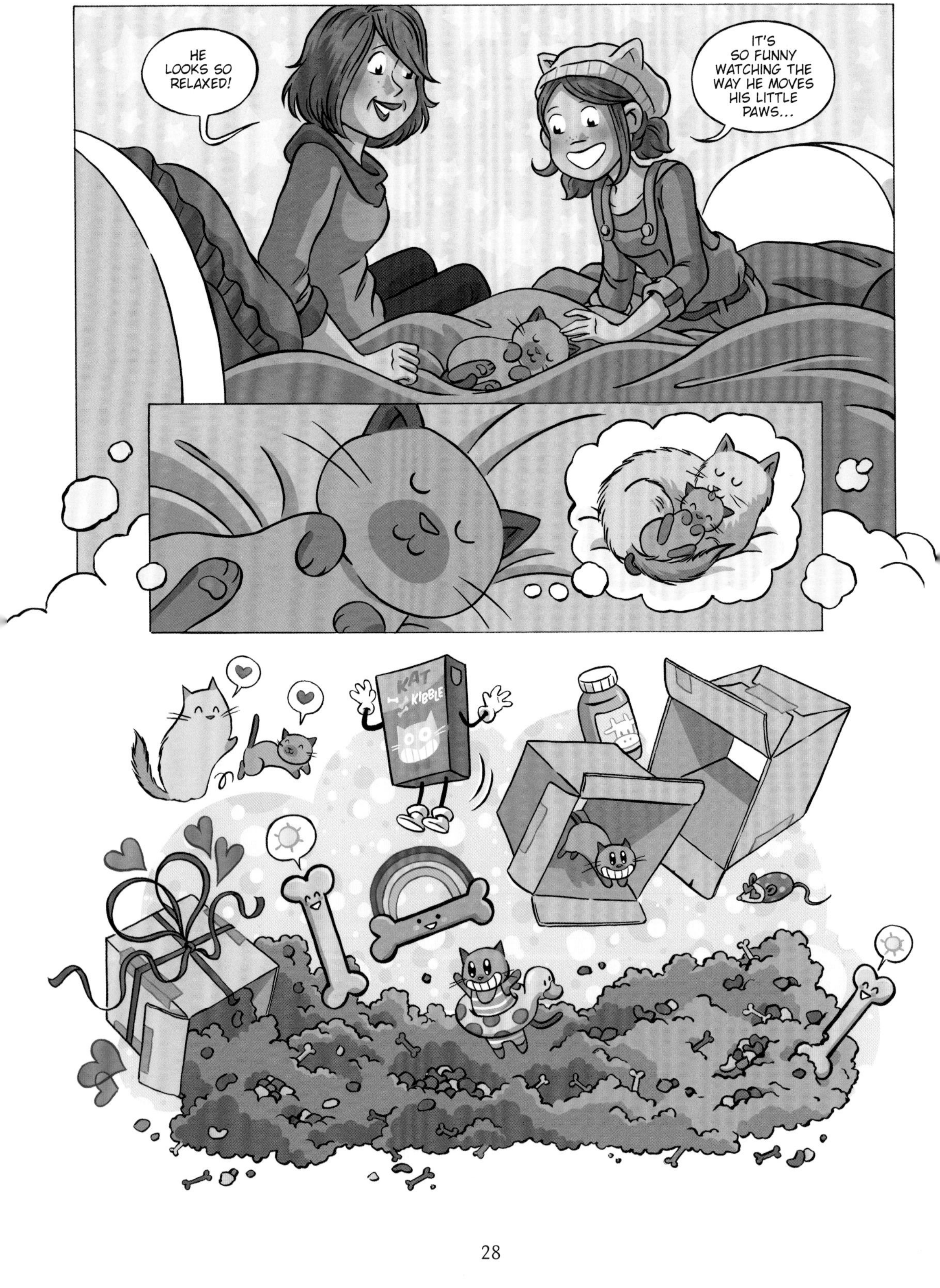
HE LOOKS SO RELAXED!
IT'S SO FUNNY WATCHING THE WAY HE MOVES HIS LITTLE PAWS...
KAT KIBBLE

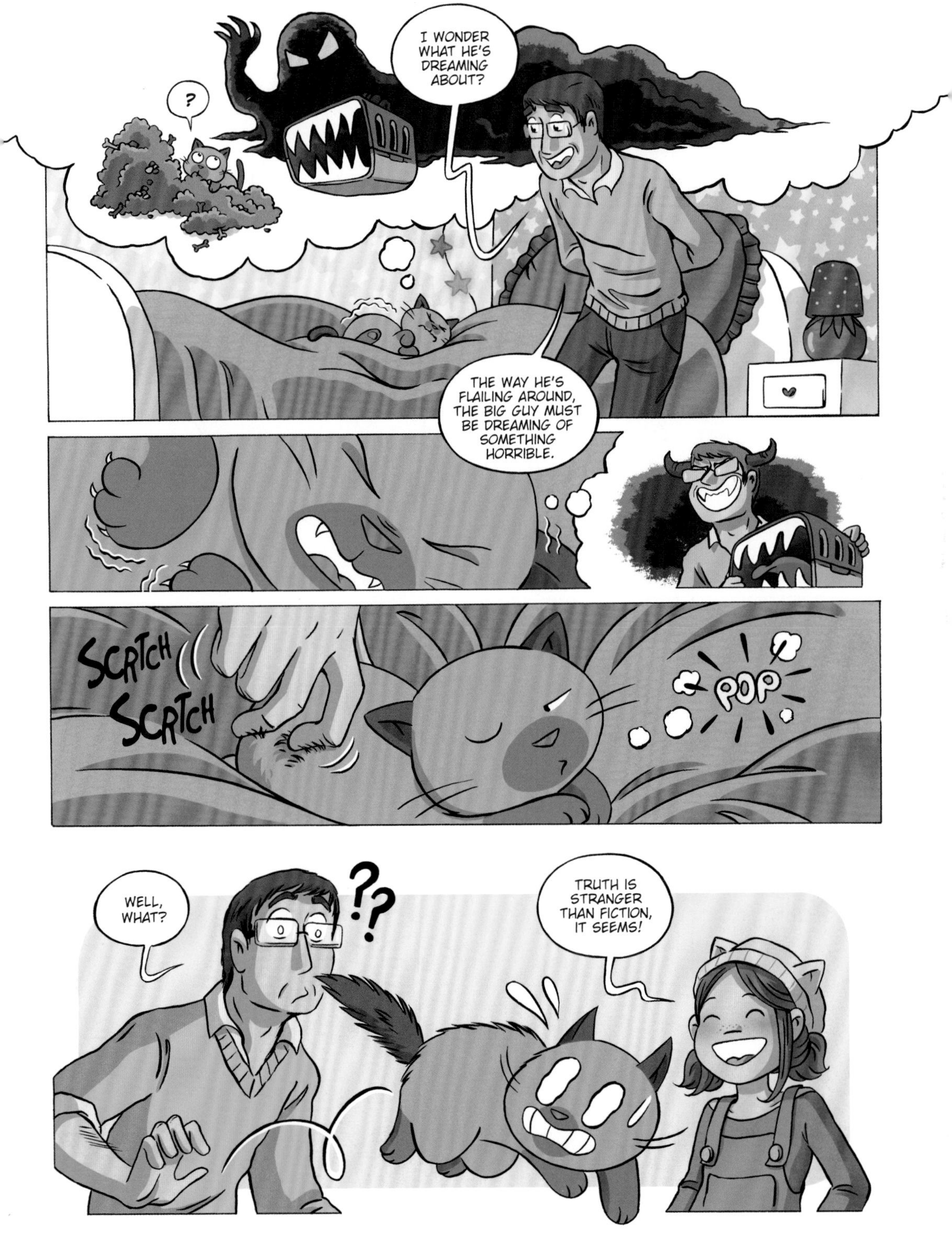
I WONDER WHAT HE'S DREAMING ABOUT?
?
THE WAY HE'S FLAILING AROUND, THE BIG GUY MUST BE DREAMING OF SOMETHING HORRIBLE.
SCRTCH SCRTCH
POP
WELL, WHAT?
??
TRUTH IS STRANGER THAN FICTION, IT SEEMS!

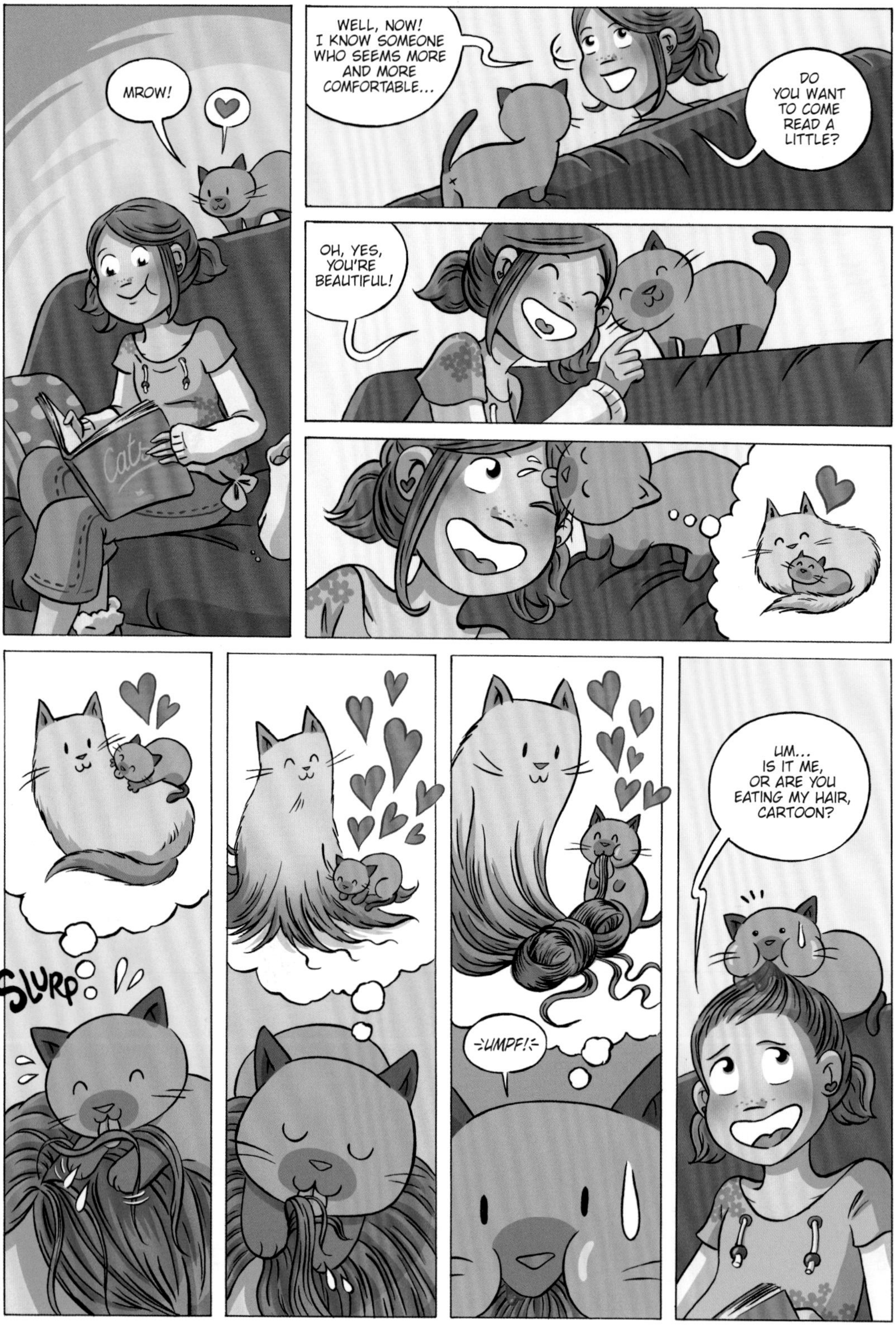
MROW!
WELL, NOW! I KNOW SOMEONE WHO SEEMS MORE AND MORE COMFORTABLE...
DO YOU WANT TO COME READ A LITTLE?
OH, YES, YOU'RE BEAUTIFUL!
SLURP
-UMPF!-
UM... IS IT ME, OR ARE YOU EATING MY HAIR, CARTOON?

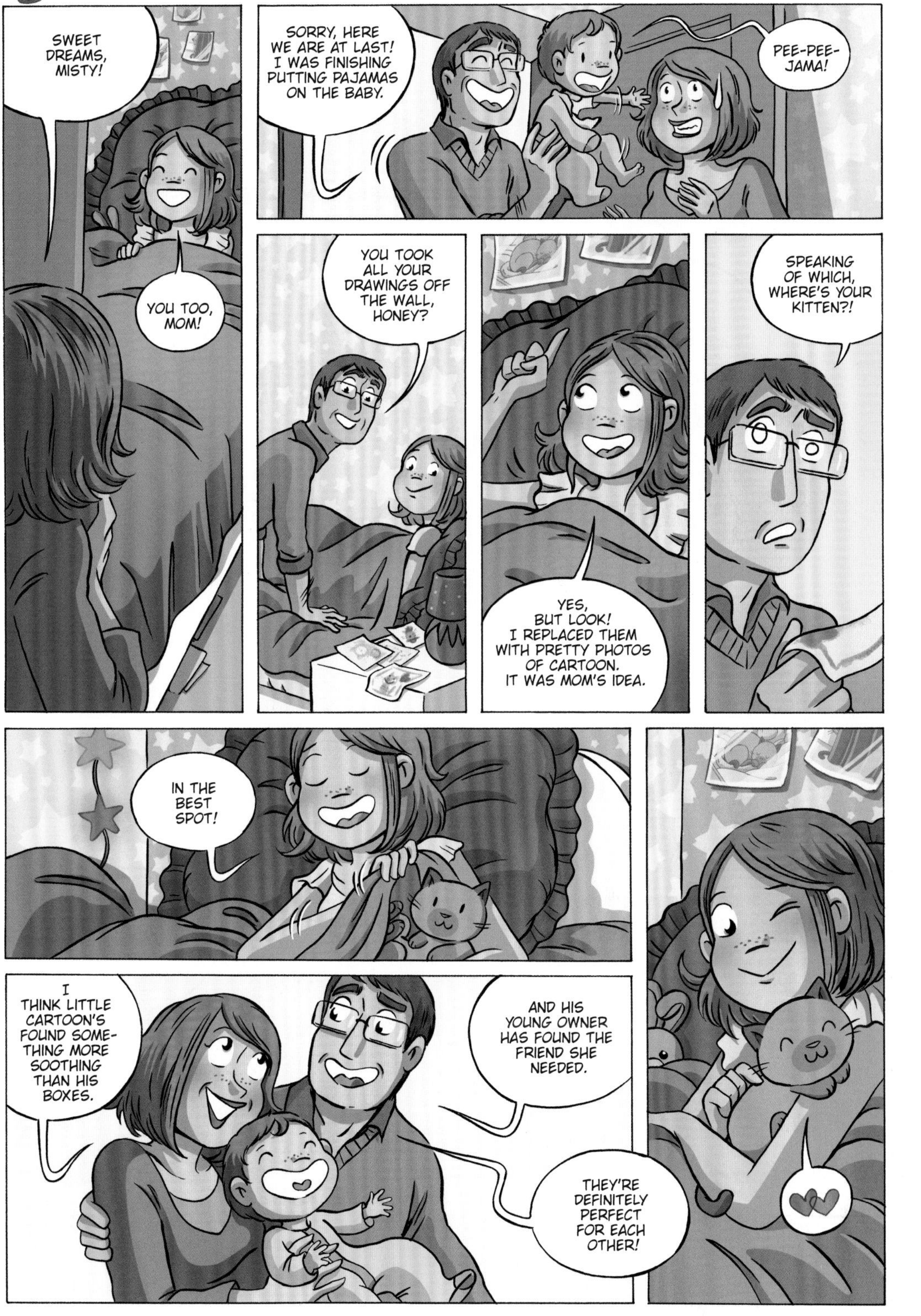
SWEET DREAMS, MISTY!
YOU TOO, MOM!
SORRY, HERE WE ARE AT LAST! I WAS FINISHING PUTTING PAJAMAS ON THE BABY.
PEE-PEE-JAMA!
YOU TOOK ALL YOUR DRAWINGS OFF THE WALL, HONEY?
YES, BUT LOOK! I REPLACED THEM WITH PRETTY PHOTOS OF CARTOON. IT WAS MOM'S IDEA.
SPEAKING OF WHICH, WHERE'S YOUR KITTEN?!
IN THE BEST SPOT!
I THINK LITTLE CARTOON'S FOUND SOME-THING MORE SOOTHING THAN HIS BOXES.
AND HIS YOUNG OWNER HAS FOUND THE FRIEND SHE NEEDED.
THEY'RE DEFINITELY PERFECT FOR EACH OTHER!

tips from Chloe

Welcoming a Kitten to Your Home

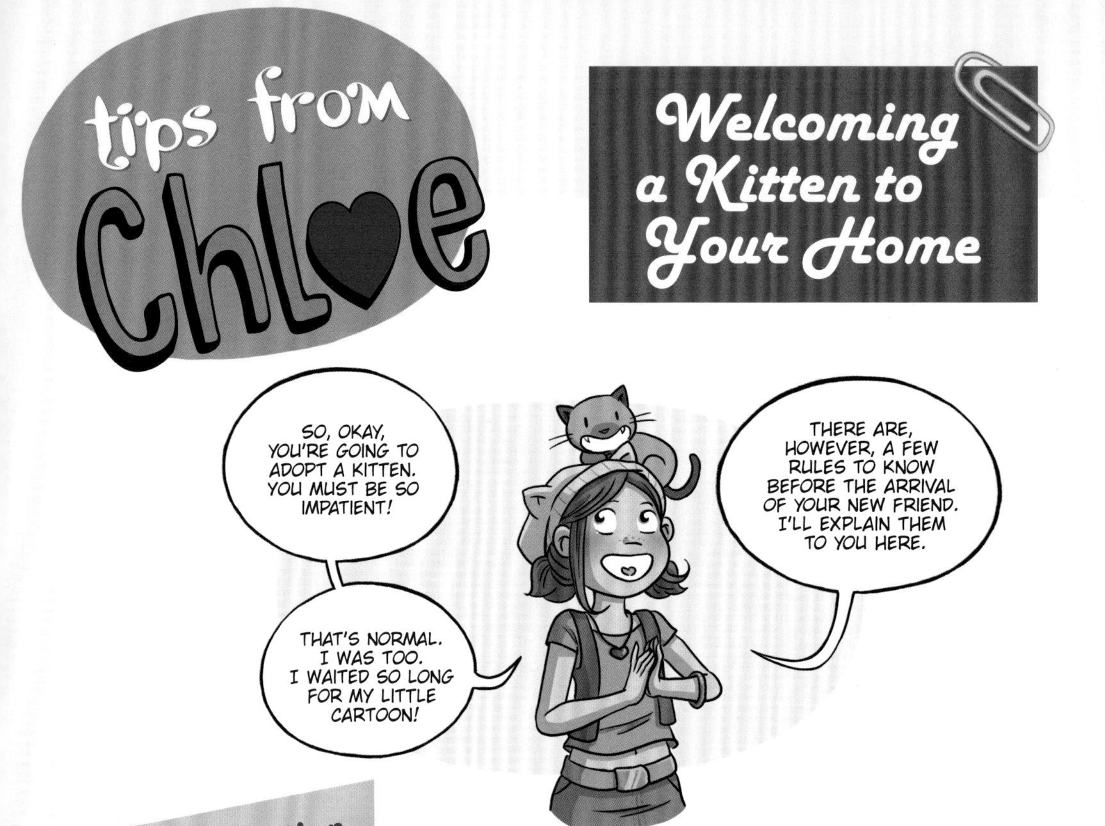
SO, OKAY, YOU'RE GOING TO ADOPT A KITTEN. YOU MUST BE SO IMPATIENT!
THAT'S NORMAL. I WAS TOO. I WAITED SO LONG FOR MY LITTLE CARTOON!
THERE ARE, HOWEVER, A FEW RULES TO KNOW BEFORE THE ARRIVAL OF YOUR NEW FRIEND. I'LL EXPLAIN THEM TO YOU HERE.

Transportation by Car

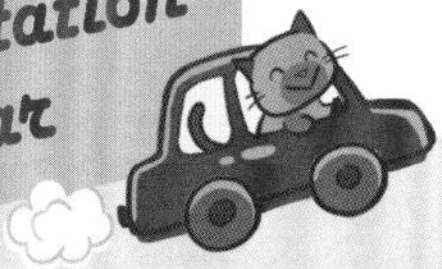

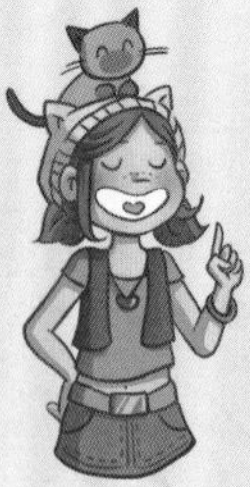

A little animal can't, of course, travel loose. It would be dangerous for the cat and not easy for you. Whatever your means of transportation, plan to bring a cat carrier! There are different models of them, you'll have plenty of choices.

If you don't have a cat carrier available, however, you can use a box as a temporary solution. All you have to do then is close it carefully. Most of all, don't forget to punch ventilation holes in it so your kitten can breathe.

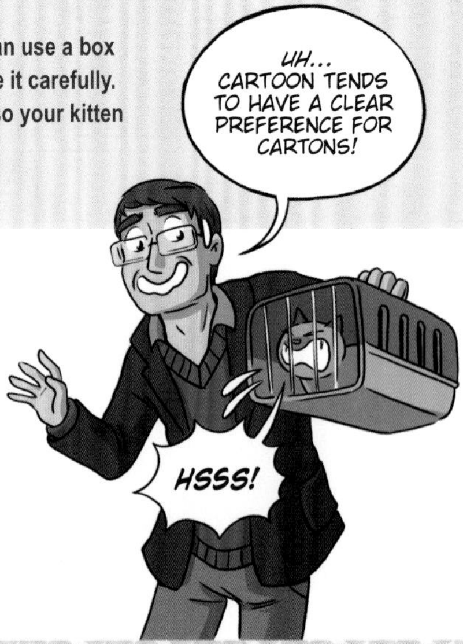
UH... CARTOON TENDS TO HAVE A CLEAR PREFERENCE FOR CARTONS!
HSSS!

A Bit of Advice:
Try to make your cat's carrier as comfortable as possible; he'll be more relaxed.

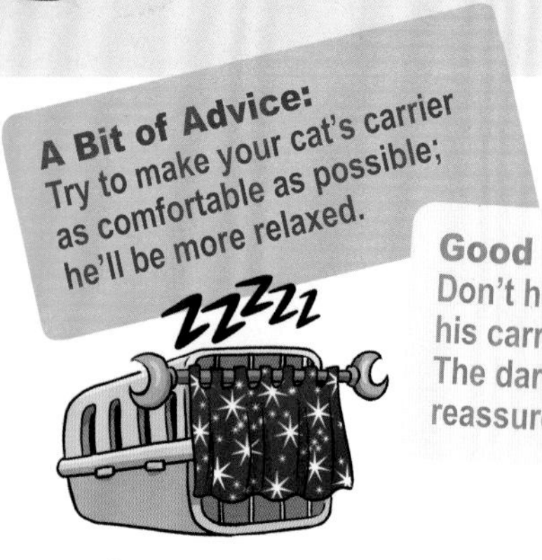
ZZZZZ

Good to Know:
Don't hesitate to cover his carrier partially. The darkness will reassure him.

The new environment

Once your kitten arrives, don't leave him by himself the first few days. Although people often think they've checked everything, you still might have missed something potentially dangerous…

If you live in a big house like I do, you can limit him to only one room or two, till he gets his bearings. It'll be less stressful and more reassuring for him!

A Bit of Advice: If possible, welcome your kitten to your home on a weekend or during vacation, that way you'll be more available.

Good to Know: Set up his little corner in a calm, warm area. There's nothing better for his well-being.

IT WAS A MUST AT OUR HOME! I THINK THE BIG GUY IS BEING DOMINATED BY THE LITTLE GUY…

AAAAH!

Feeding and the litter box

As for dry cat food and litter, don't complicate your life! It's important not to upset your new friend's habits. So, choose the products he used at his previous home. And most important of all, don't forget to make sure he always has water available!

Organization-wise, plan to put distance between his litterbox and food dish, so that it doesn't bother him.

A Bit of Advice: Try to change out the water regularly, at least two or three times a day. Cats have a delicate palate and appreciate fresh water!

Good to Know: Contrary to what people imagine, cow's milk is indigestible for our four-legged friends. Nevertheless, you can occasionally give him some to make him happy (by diluting it with a bit of water, for instance). Onion, garlic, apricots, chocolate, and parsley are also off-limits, since they're toxic for cats.

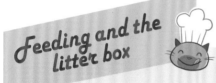

AT FIRST GLANCE, LOOKS LIKE THAT KIBBLE IS GOOD.

÷BURP!÷

Bedding

The bedding choice is of great importance for the kitten's comfort and safety.

A wicker basket, a box or another sort of container adapted to his size, and a fluffy layer or cushion will usually do the trick.

A Bit of Advice: Don't worry if your kitten chooses what seems to be the best bedding for him. It's also a question of taste, after all!

Good to Know: Cats sleep a lot, around sixteen hours per day for an adult, around twenty hours for a kitten.

SOMEBODY'S LIVING THE GOOD LIFE HERE!

Playtime

So your pet can flourish in the best conditions, he needs to be stimulated and have the means to express himself.

Whether you've bought or made them yourself, plan to put scratching posts, a cat tree, and other toys at his disposal, in order to arouse his curiosity!

A Bit of Advice: A kitten being a kitten, you must be conscious he's bound to do naughty things. So, relax about it, it's just stuff after all!

Good to Know: Playing is excellent for your cat's health and also lets him express his natural hunting instinct.

IT DOESN'T WORK EVERY TIME, THOUGH!

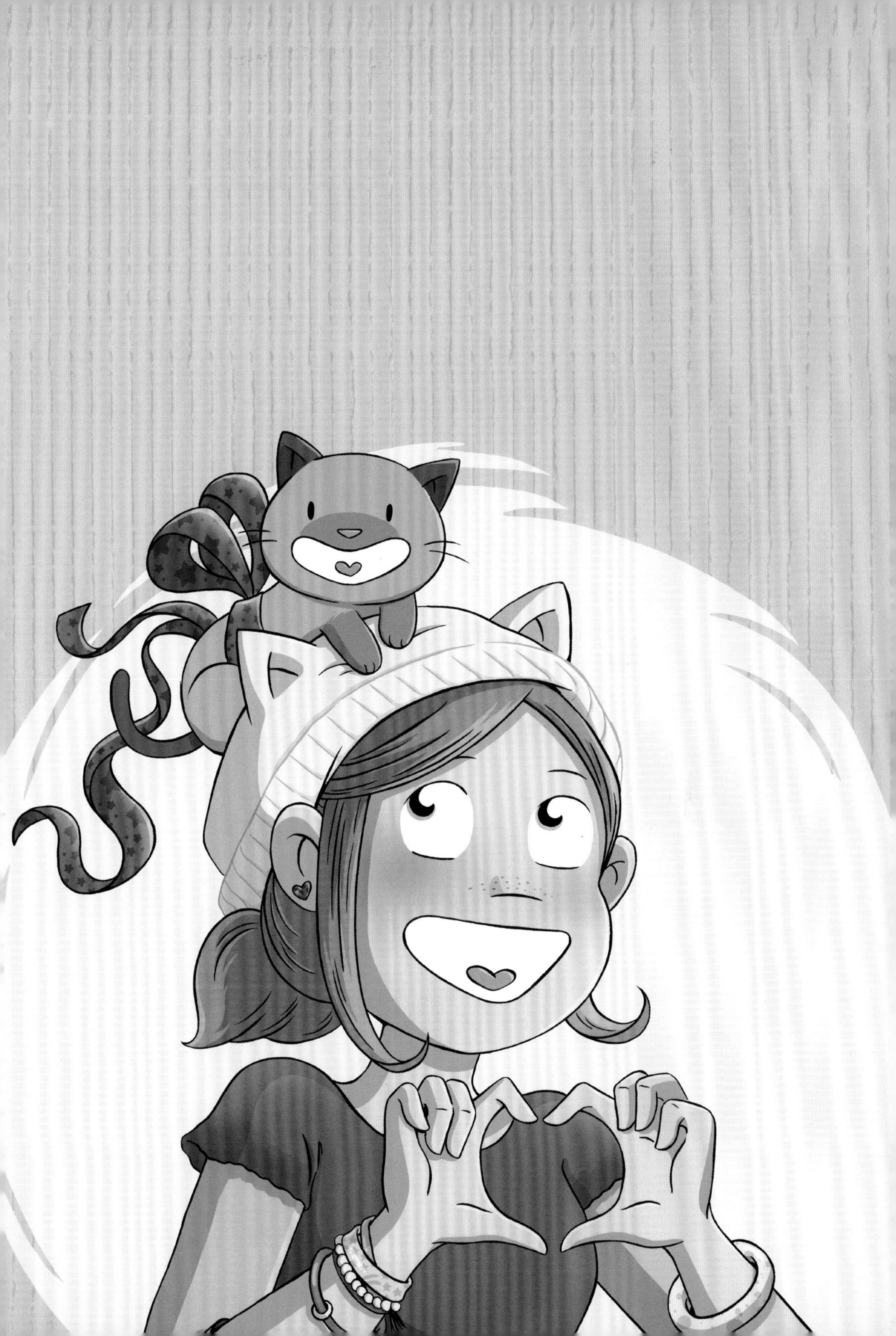

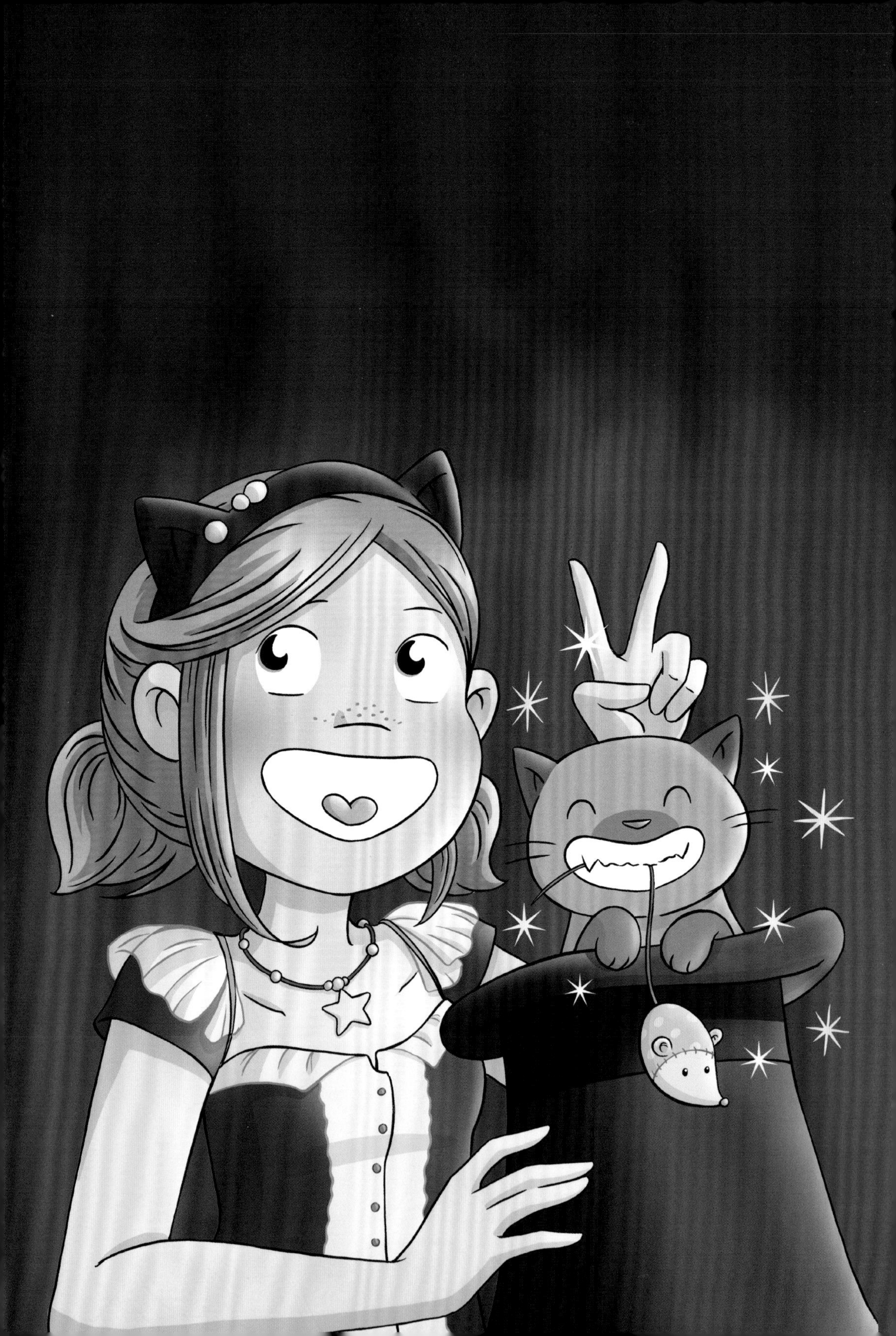

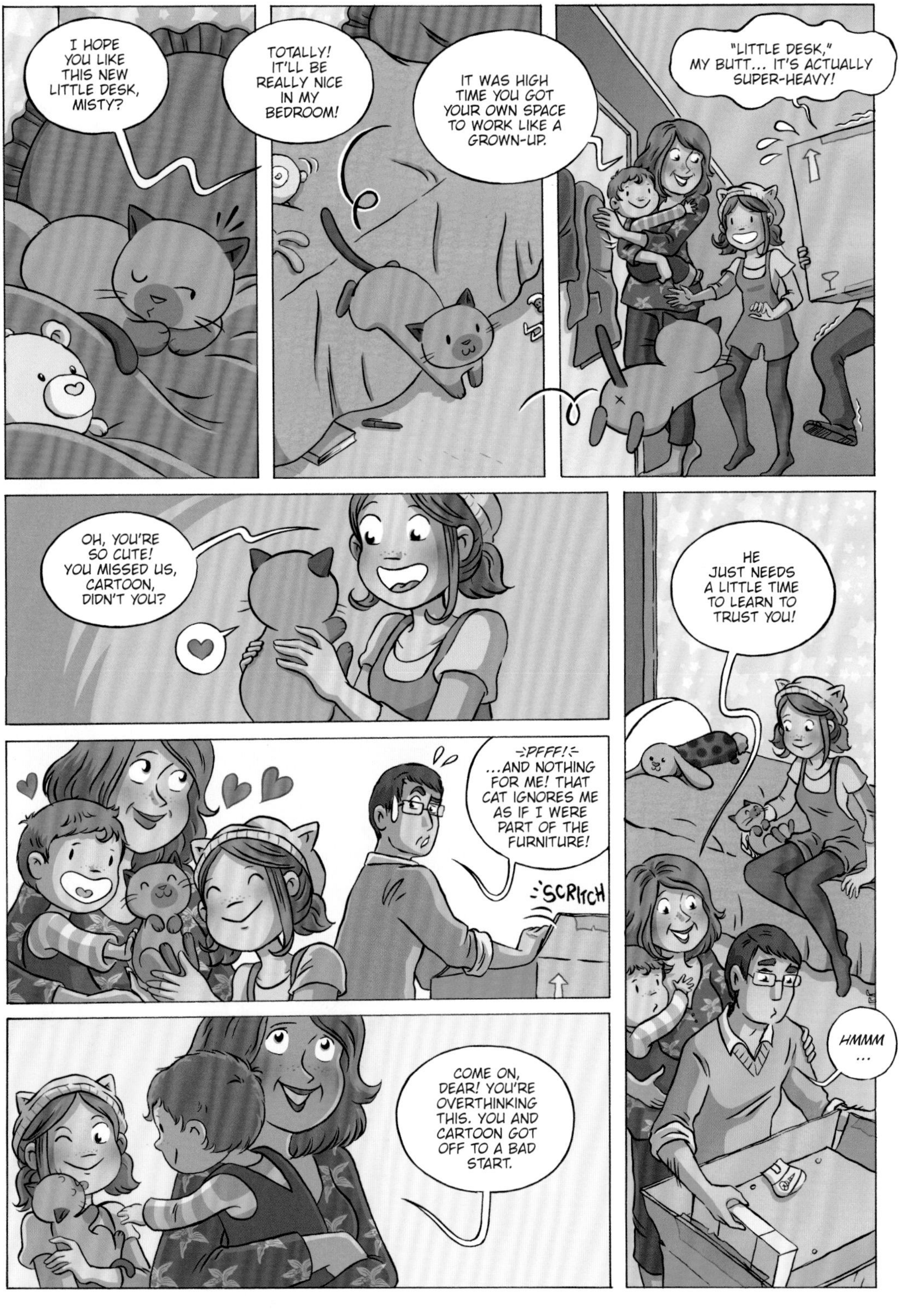
I HOPE YOU LIKE THIS NEW LITTLE DESK, MISTY?
TOTALLY! IT'LL BE REALLY NICE IN MY BEDROOM!
IT WAS HIGH TIME YOU GOT YOUR OWN SPACE TO WORK LIKE A GROWN-UP.
"LITTLE DESK," MY BUTT... IT'S ACTUALLY SUPER-HEAVY!
OH, YOU'RE SO CUTE! YOU MISSED US, CARTOON, DIDN'T YOU?
HE JUST NEEDS A LITTLE TIME TO LEARN TO TRUST YOU!
PFFF!
...AND NOTHING FOR ME! THAT CAT IGNORES ME AS IF I WERE PART OF THE FURNITURE!
SCRITCH
COME ON, DEAR! YOU'RE OVERTHINKING THIS. YOU AND CARTOON GOT OFF TO A BAD START.
HMMM ...

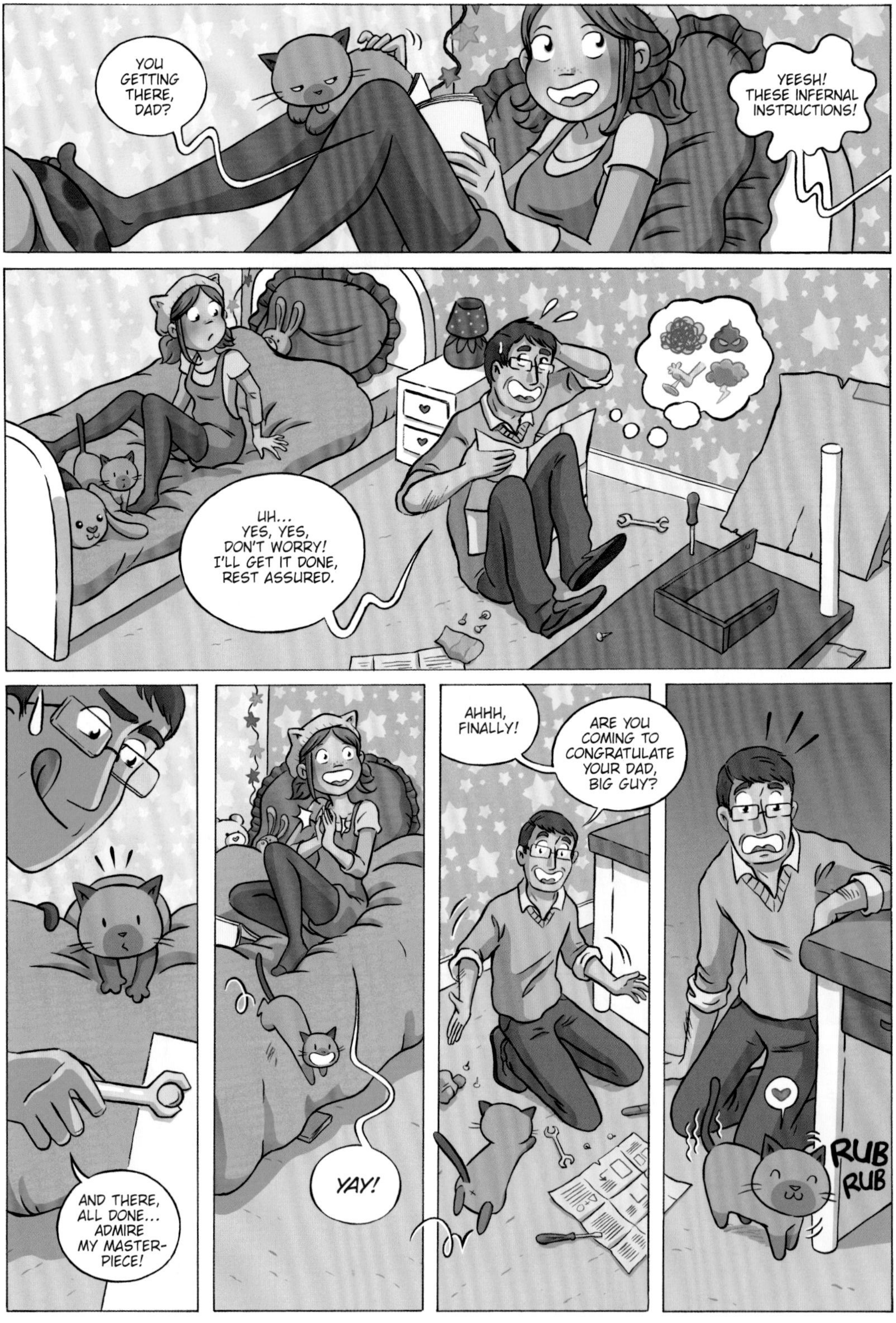
YOU GETTING THERE, DAD?
YEESH! THESE INFERNAL INSTRUCTIONS!
UH... YES, YES, DON'T WORRY! I'LL GET IT DONE, REST ASSURED.
AND THERE, ALL DONE... ADMIRE MY MASTER-PIECE!
YAY!
AHHH, FINALLY!
ARE YOU COMING TO CONGRATULATE YOUR DAD, BIG GUY?
RUB RUB

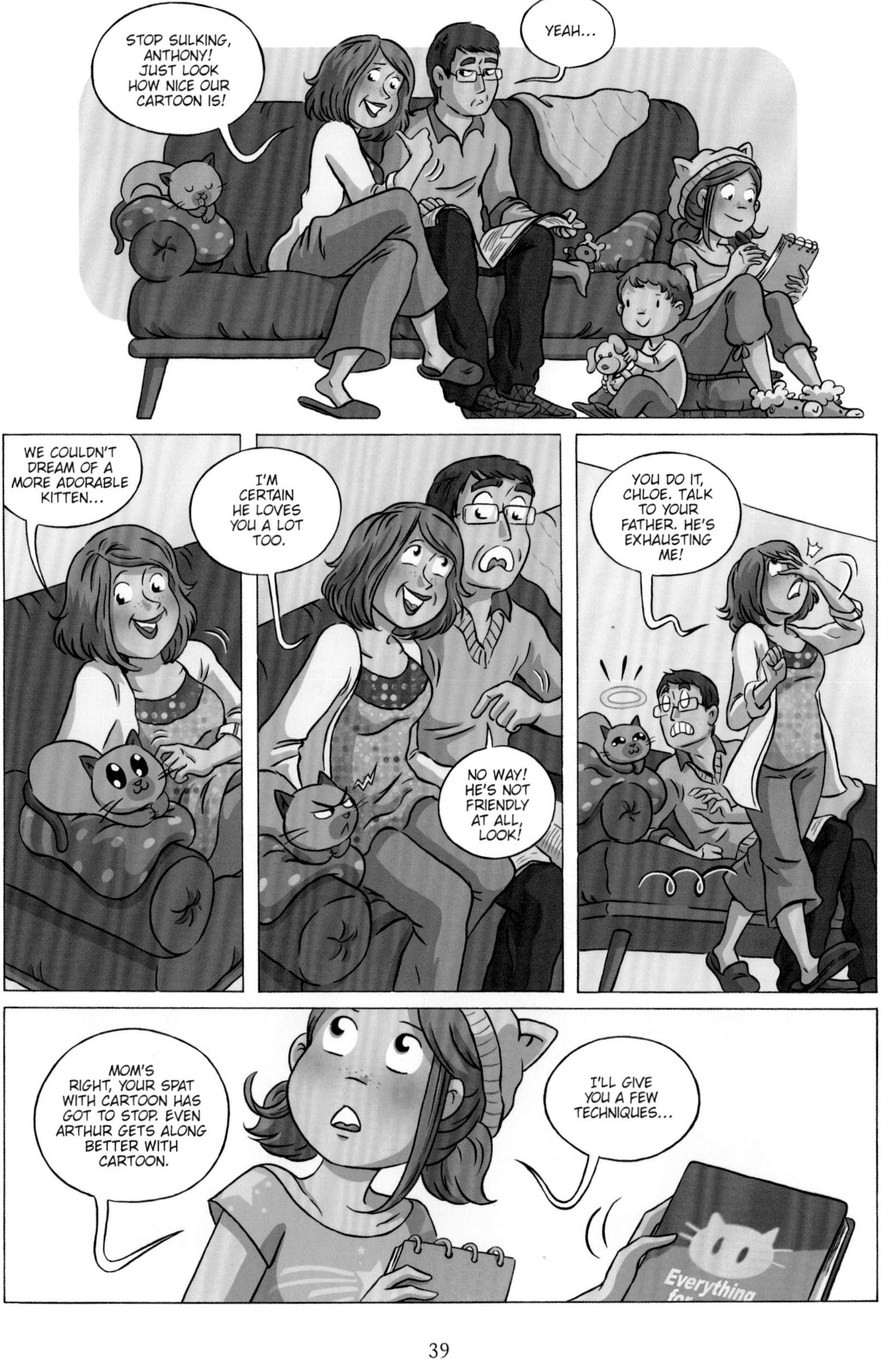
STOP SULKING, ANTHONY! JUST LOOK HOW NICE OUR CARTOON IS!
YEAH...
WE COULDN'T DREAM OF A MORE ADORABLE KITTEN...
I'M CERTAIN HE LOVES YOU A LOT TOO.
NO WAY! HE'S NOT FRIENDLY AT ALL, LOOK!
YOU DO IT, CHLOE. TALK TO YOUR FATHER. HE'S EXHAUSTING ME!
MOM'S RIGHT, YOUR SPAT WITH CARTOON HAS GOT TO STOP. EVEN ARTHUR GETS ALONG BETTER WITH CARTOON.
I'LL GIVE YOU A FEW TECHNIQUES...

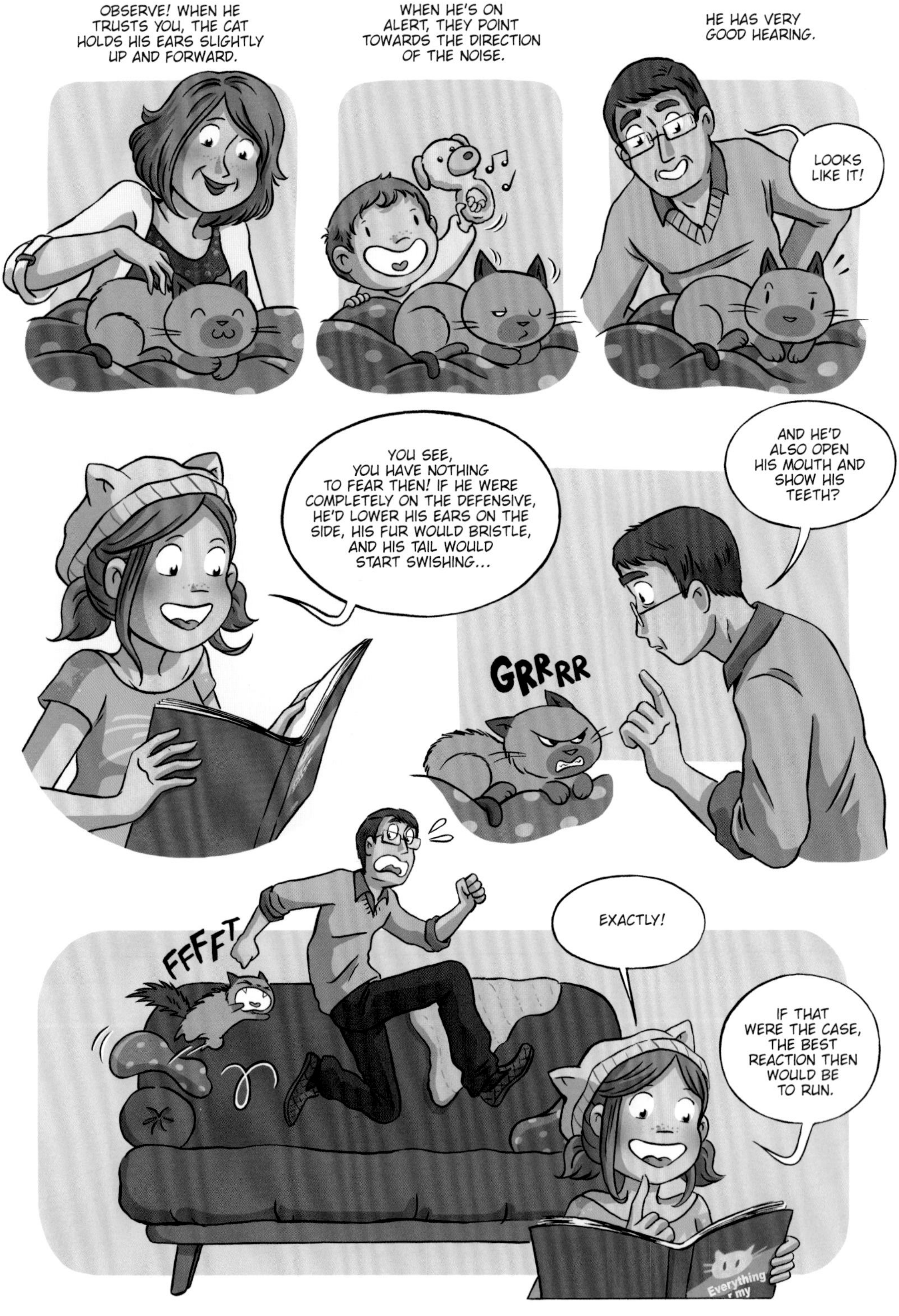
OBSERVE! WHEN HE TRUSTS YOU, THE CAT HOLDS HIS EARS SLIGHTLY UP AND FORWARD.
WHEN HE'S ON ALERT, THEY POINT TOWARDS THE DIRECTION OF THE NOISE.
HE HAS VERY GOOD HEARING.
LOOKS LIKE IT!
YOU SEE, YOU HAVE NOTHING TO FEAR THEN! IF HE WERE COMPLETELY ON THE DEFENSIVE, HE'D LOWER HIS EARS ON THE SIDE, HIS FUR WOULD BRISTLE, AND HIS TAIL WOULD START SWISHING...
AND HE'D ALSO OPEN HIS MOUTH AND SHOW HIS TEETH?
GRRRR
FFFFT
EXACTLY!
IF THAT WERE THE CASE, THE BEST REACTION THEN WOULD BE TO RUN.

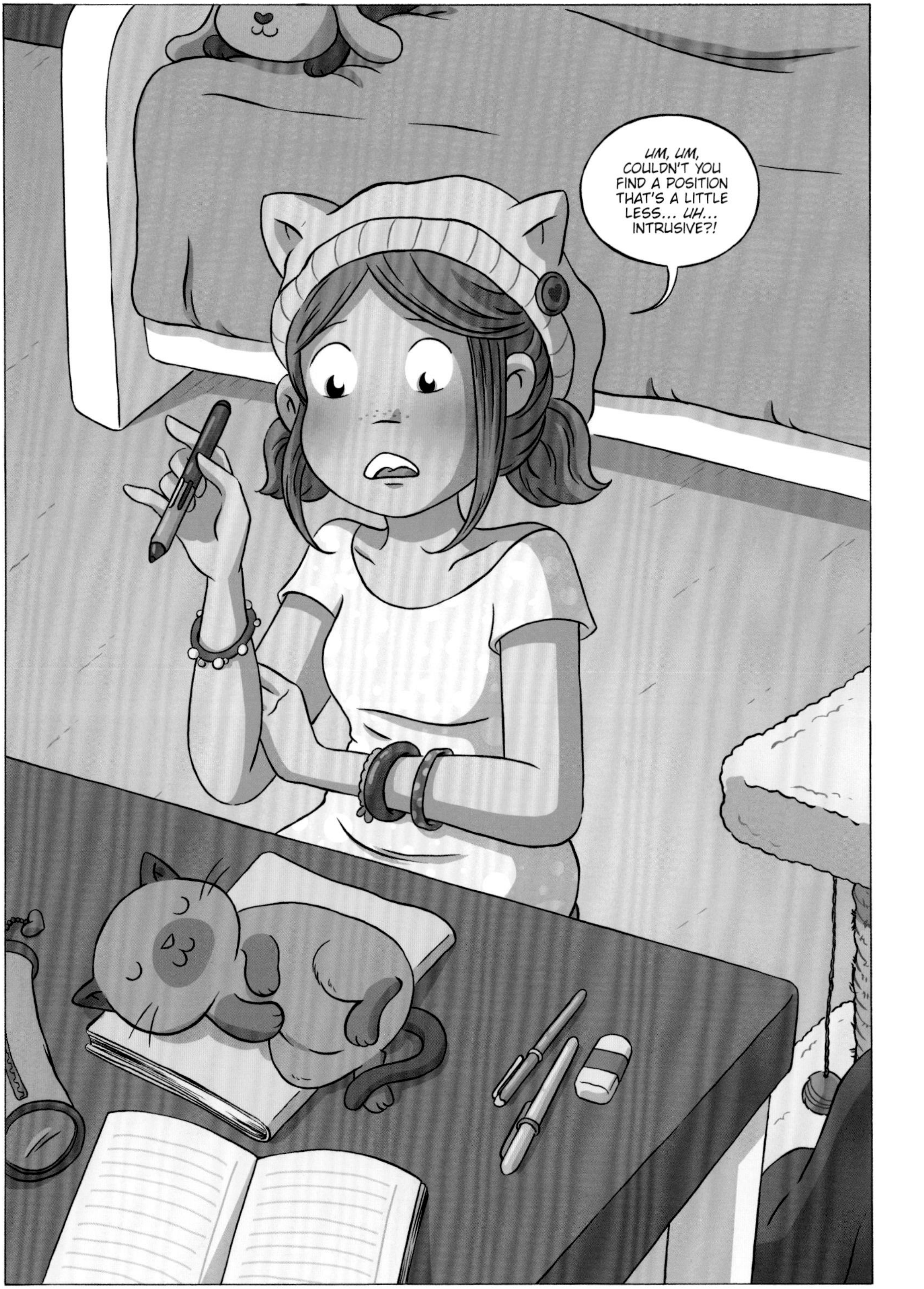
UM, UM, COULDN'T YOU FIND A POSITION THAT'S A LITTLE LESS... UH... INTRUSIVE?!

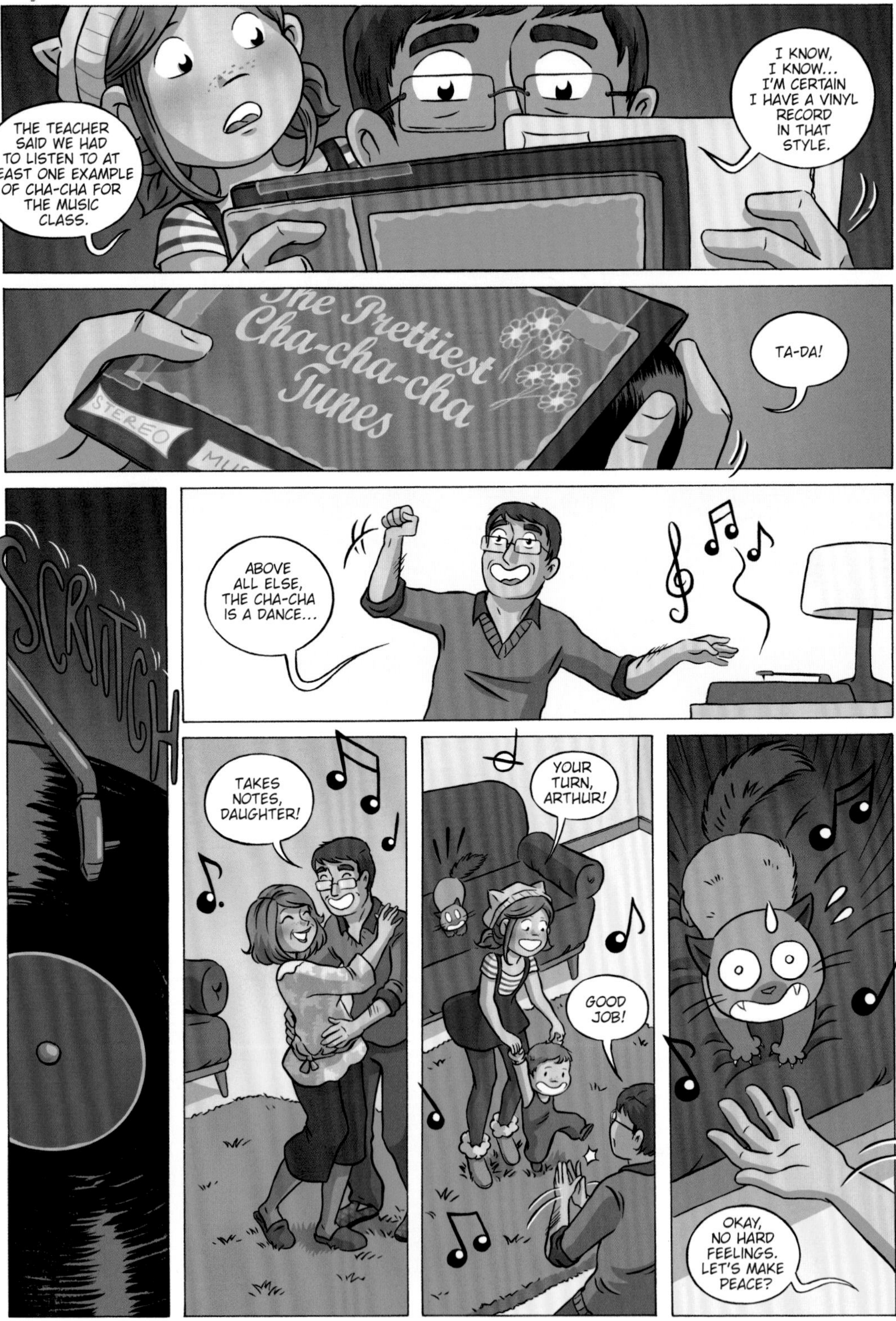
THE TEACHER SAID WE HAD TO LISTEN TO AT LEAST ONE EXAMPLE OF CHA-CHA FOR THE MUSIC CLASS.
I KNOW, I KNOW... I'M CERTAIN I HAVE A VINYL RECORD IN THAT STYLE.
The Prettiest Cha-cha-cha Tunes
STEREO
TA-DA!
SCRITCH
ABOVE ALL ELSE, THE CHA-CHA IS A DANCE...
TAKES NOTES, DAUGHTER!
YOUR TURN, ARTHUR!
GOOD JOB!
OKAY, NO HARD FEELINGS. LET'S MAKE PEACE?

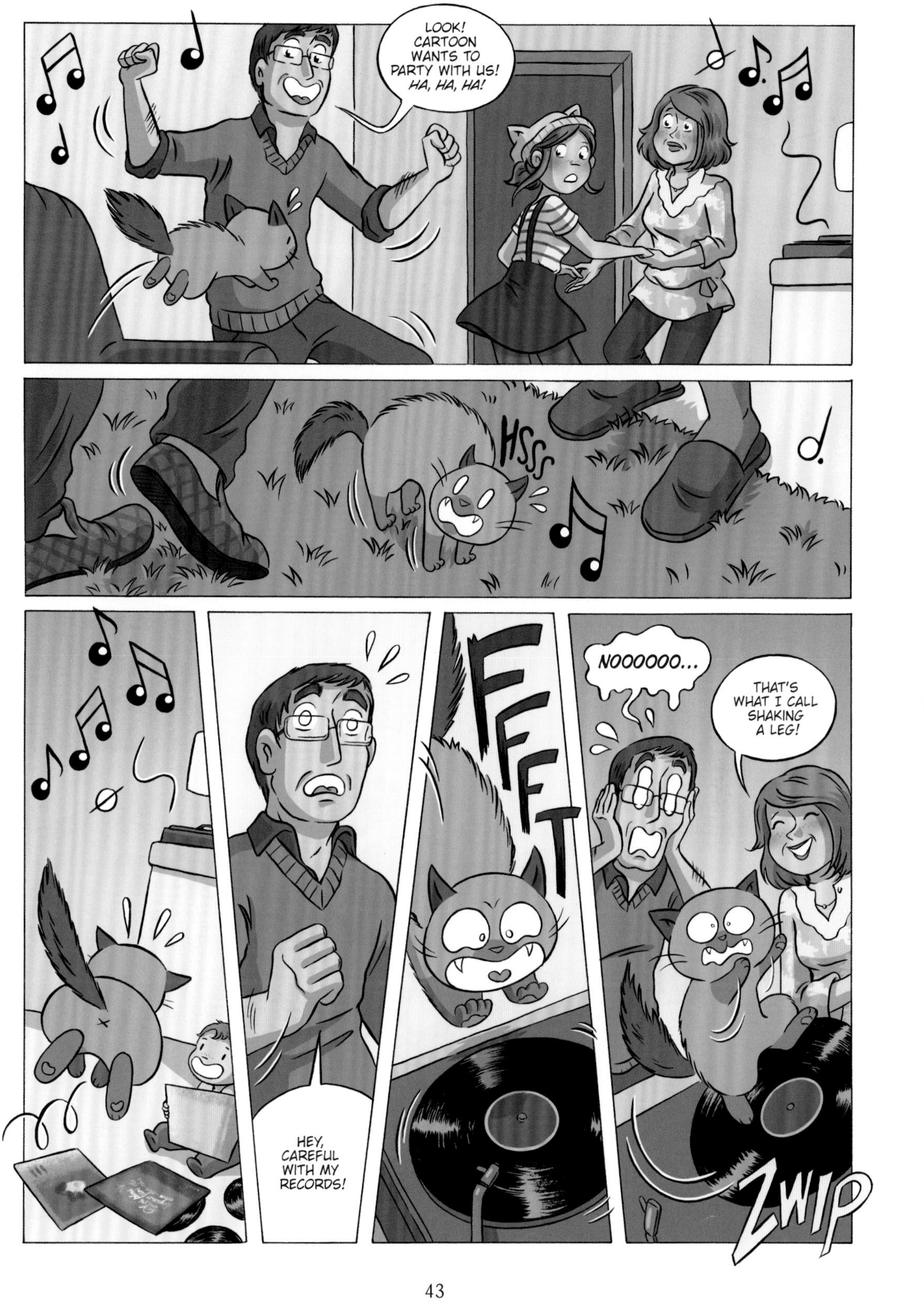
LOOK! CARTOON WANTS TO PARTY WITH US! HA, HA, HA!
HSSS
FFFT
NOOOOOO...
THAT'S WHAT I CALL SHAKING A LEG!
HEY, CAREFUL WITH MY RECORDS!
ZWIP

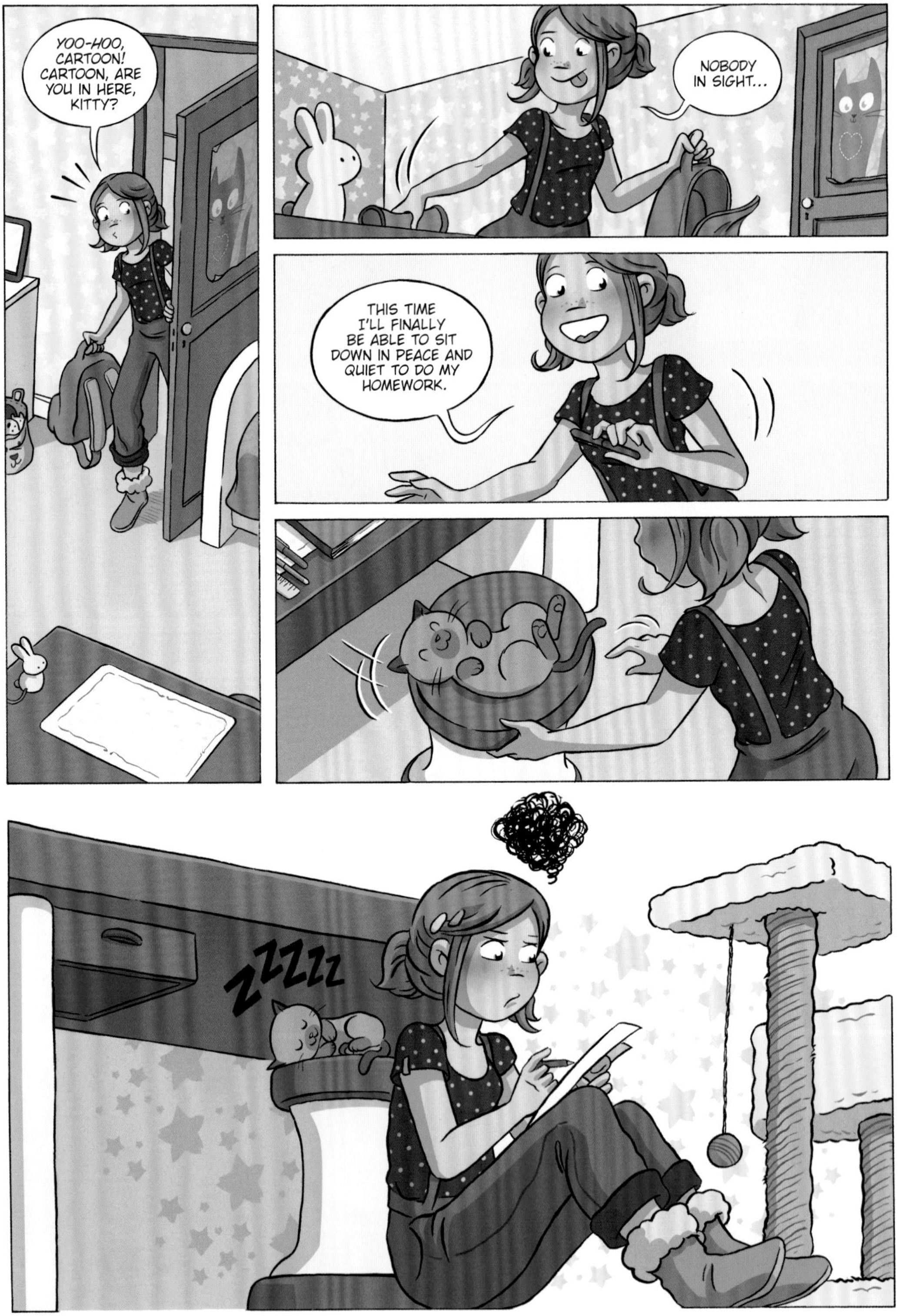
YOO-HOO, CARTOON! CARTOON, ARE YOU IN HERE, KITTY?
NOBODY IN SIGHT...
THIS TIME I'LL FINALLY BE ABLE TO SIT DOWN IN PEACE AND QUIET TO DO MY HOMEWORK.
ZZZZZ

Shhhh!

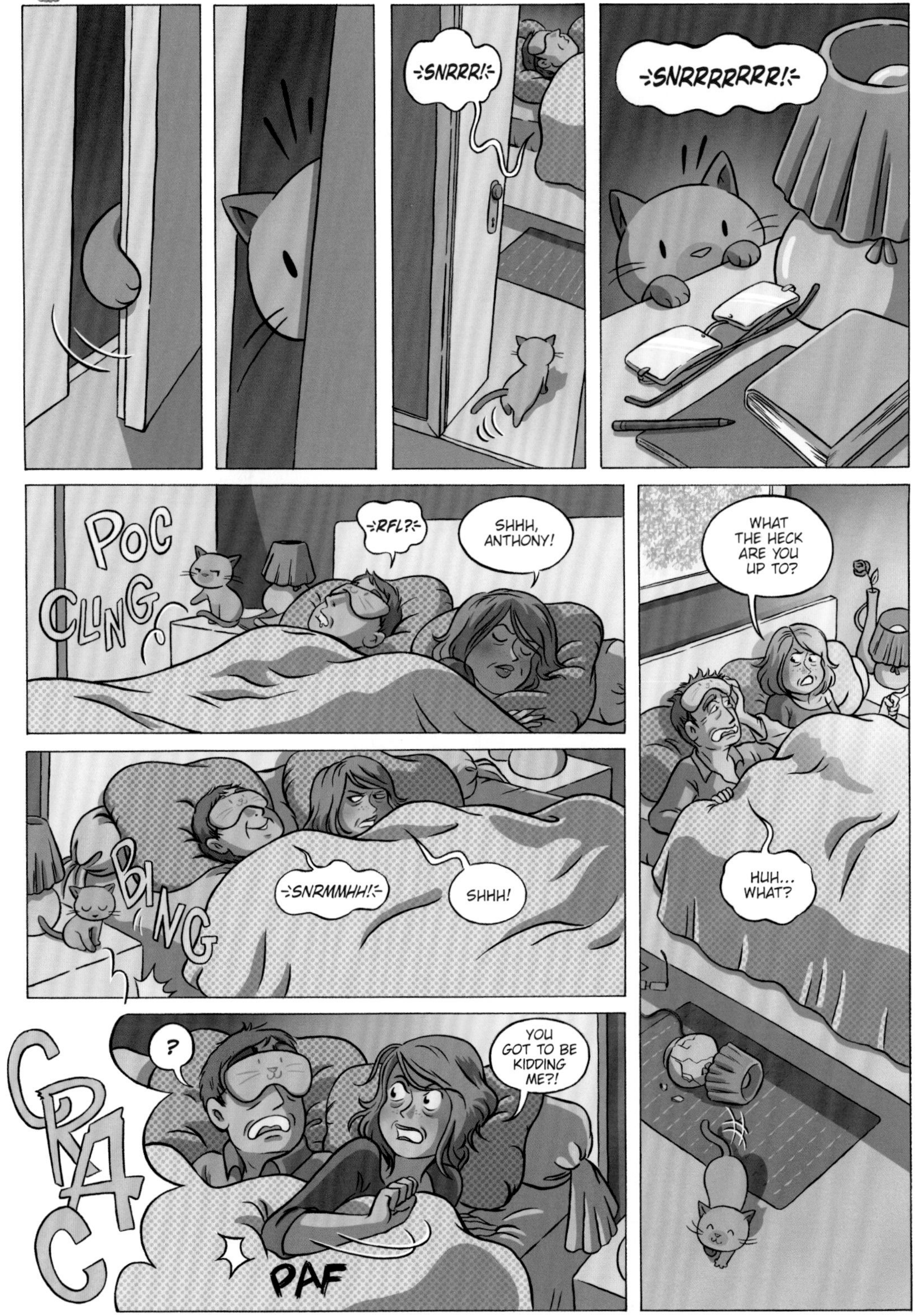

SNRRR!
SNRRRRRRR!
POC
CLING
RFL?
SHHH, ANTHONY!
WHAT THE HECK ARE YOU UP TO?
HUH... WHAT?
BING
SNRMMHH!
SHHH!
CRAC
?
YOU GOT TO BE KIDDING ME?!
PAF

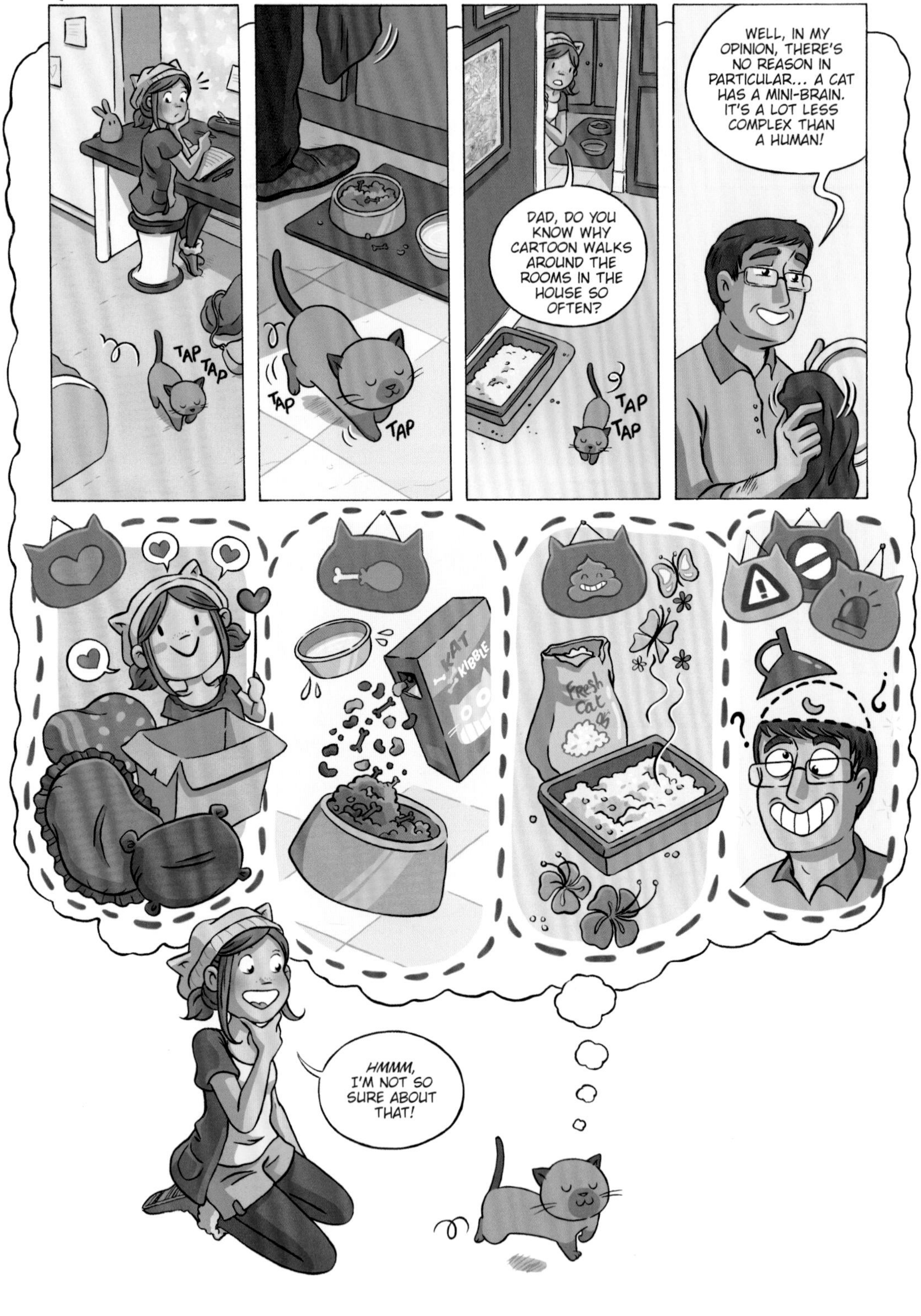
TAP
TAP
TAP
TAP
DAD, DO YOU KNOW WHY CARTOON WALKS AROUND THE ROOMS IN THE HOUSE SO OFTEN?
TAP
TAP
WELL, IN MY OPINION, THERE'S NO REASON IN PARTICULAR... A CAT HAS A MINI-BRAIN. IT'S A LOT LESS COMPLEX THAN A HUMAN!
KAT KIBBLE
FRESH CAT
HMMM, I'M NOT SO SURE ABOUT THAT!

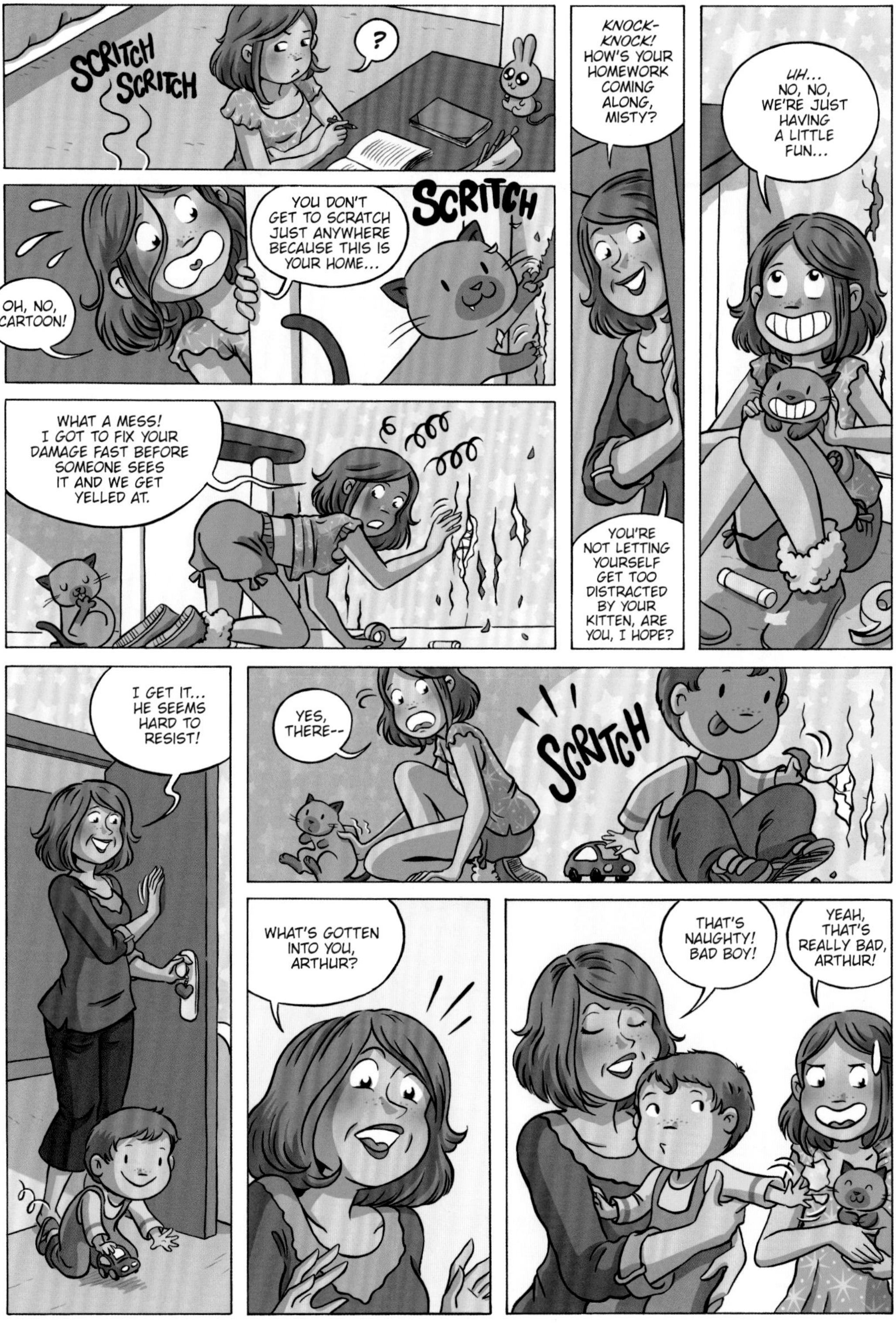
SCRITCH SCRITCH
?
KNOCK-KNOCK! HOW'S YOUR HOMEWORK COMING ALONG, MISTY?
UH... NO, NO, WE'RE JUST HAVING A LITTLE FUN...
OH, NO, CARTOON!
YOU DON'T GET TO SCRATCH JUST ANYWHERE BECAUSE THIS IS YOUR HOME...
SCRITCH
WHAT A MESS! I GOT TO FIX YOUR DAMAGE FAST BEFORE SOMEONE SEES IT AND WE GET YELLED AT.
YOU'RE NOT LETTING YOURSELF GET TOO DISTRACTED BY YOUR KITTEN, ARE YOU, I HOPE?
I GET IT... HE SEEMS HARD TO RESIST!
YES, THERE--
SCRITCH
WHAT'S GOTTEN INTO YOU, ARTHUR?
THAT'S NAUGHTY! BAD BOY!
YEAH, THAT'S REALLY BAD, ARTHUR!

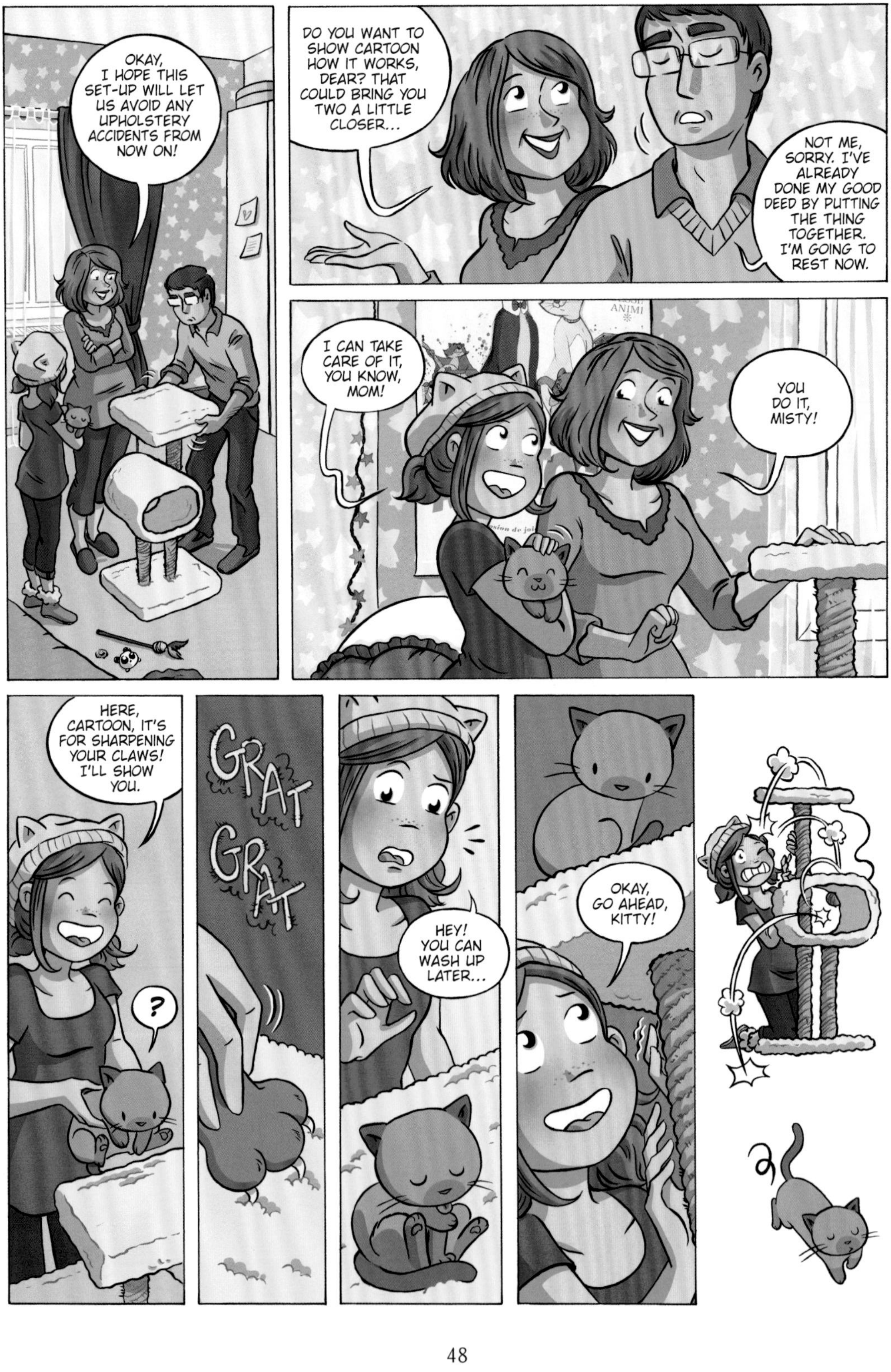
OKAY, I HOPE THIS SET-UP WILL LET US AVOID ANY UPHOLSTERY ACCIDENTS FROM NOW ON!
DO YOU WANT TO SHOW CARTOON HOW IT WORKS, DEAR? THAT COULD BRING YOU TWO A LITTLE CLOSER...
NOT ME, SORRY. I'VE ALREADY DONE MY GOOD DEED BY PUTTING THE THING TOGETHER. I'M GOING TO REST NOW.
I CAN TAKE CARE OF IT, YOU KNOW, MOM!
YOU DO IT, MISTY!
HERE, CARTOON, IT'S FOR SHARPENING YOUR CLAWS! I'LL SHOW YOU.
?
GRAT
GRAT
HEY! YOU CAN WASH UP LATER...
OKAY, GO AHEAD, KITTY!

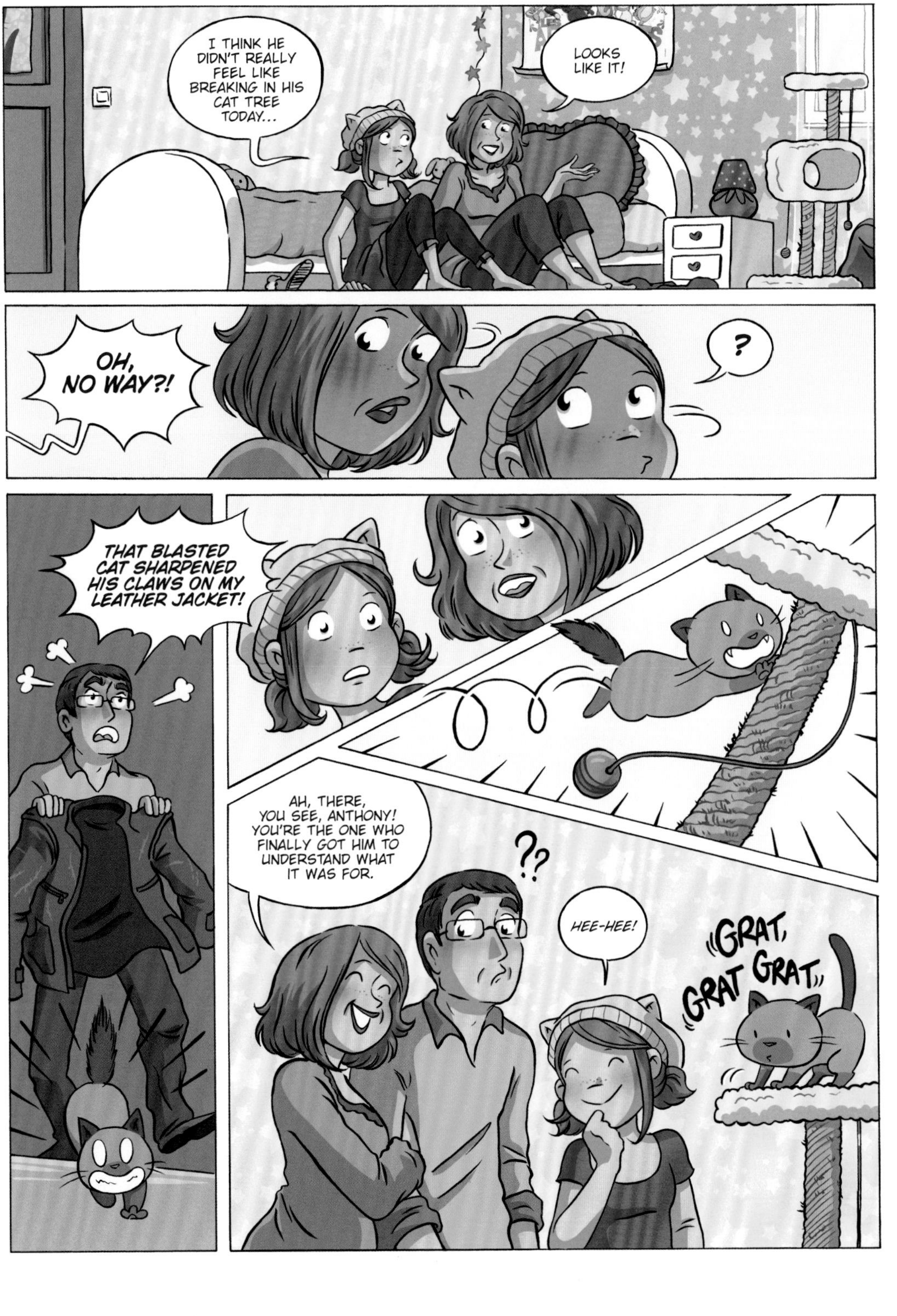
I THINK HE DIDN'T REALLY FEEL LIKE BREAKING IN HIS CAT TREE TODAY...
LOOKS LIKE IT!
OH, NO WAY?!
?
THAT BLASTED CAT SHARPENED HIS CLAWS ON MY LEATHER JACKET!
AH, THERE, YOU SEE, ANTHONY! YOU'RE THE ONE WHO FINALLY GOT HIM TO UNDERSTAND WHAT IT WAS FOR.
??
HEE-HEE!
GRAT, GRAT GRAT

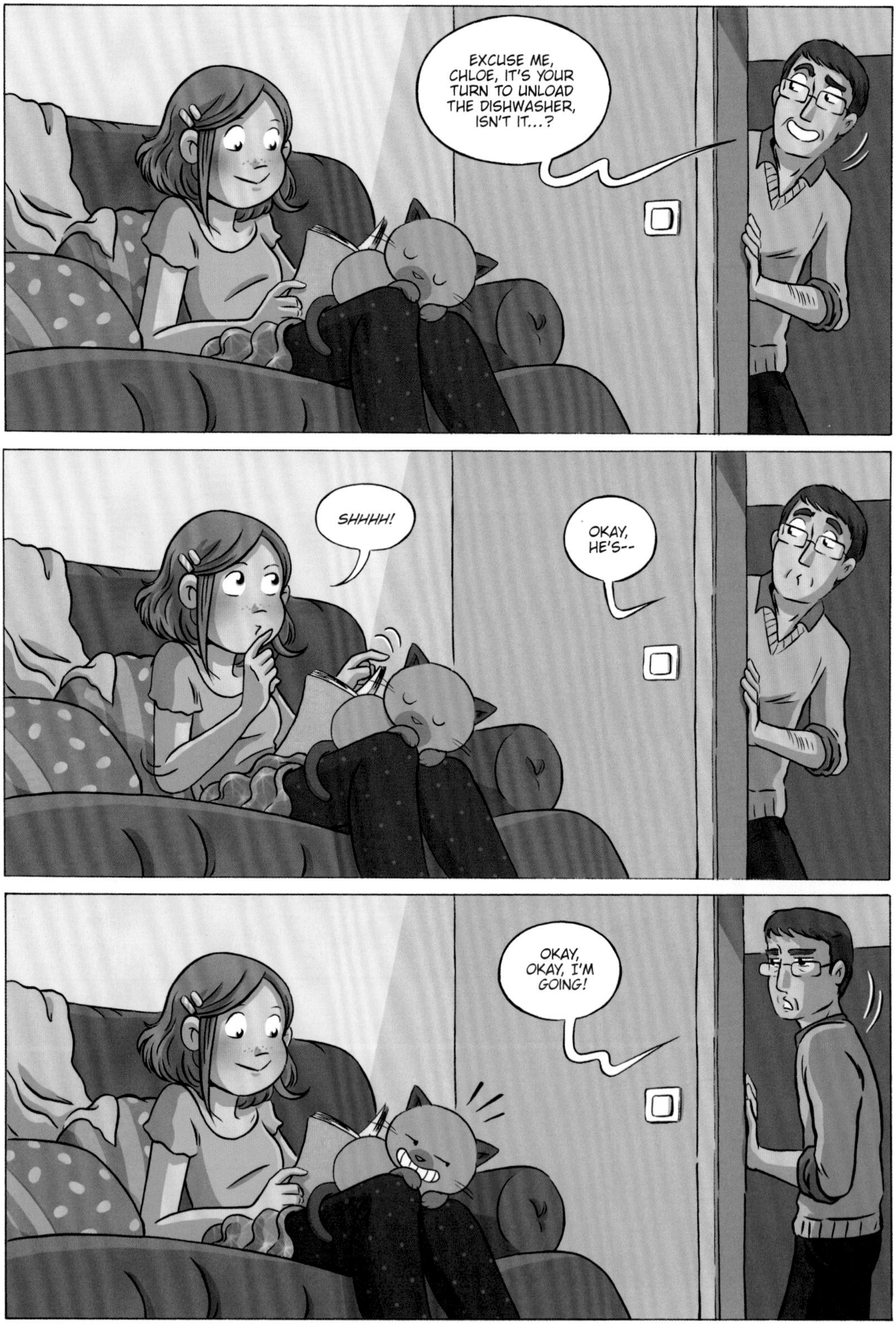
EXCUSE ME, CHLOE, IT'S YOUR TURN TO UNLOAD THE DISHWASHER, ISN'T IT...?
SHHHH!
OKAY, HE'S--
OKAY, OKAY, I'M GOING!

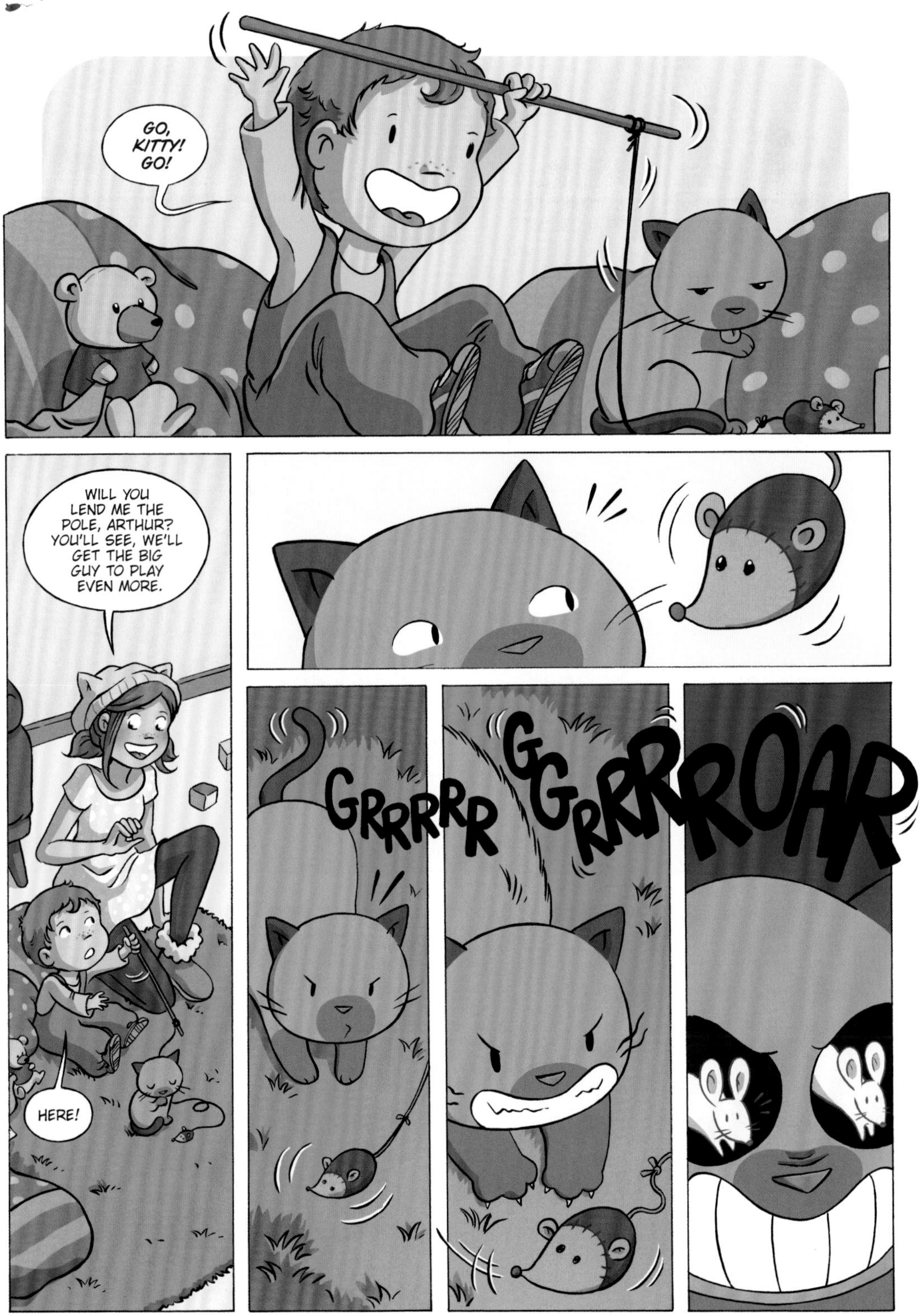
GO, KITTY! GO!
WILL YOU LEND ME THE POLE, ARTHUR? YOU'LL SEE, WE'LL GET THE BIG GUY TO PLAY EVEN MORE.
HERE!
GRRRRR
GGRRRROAR

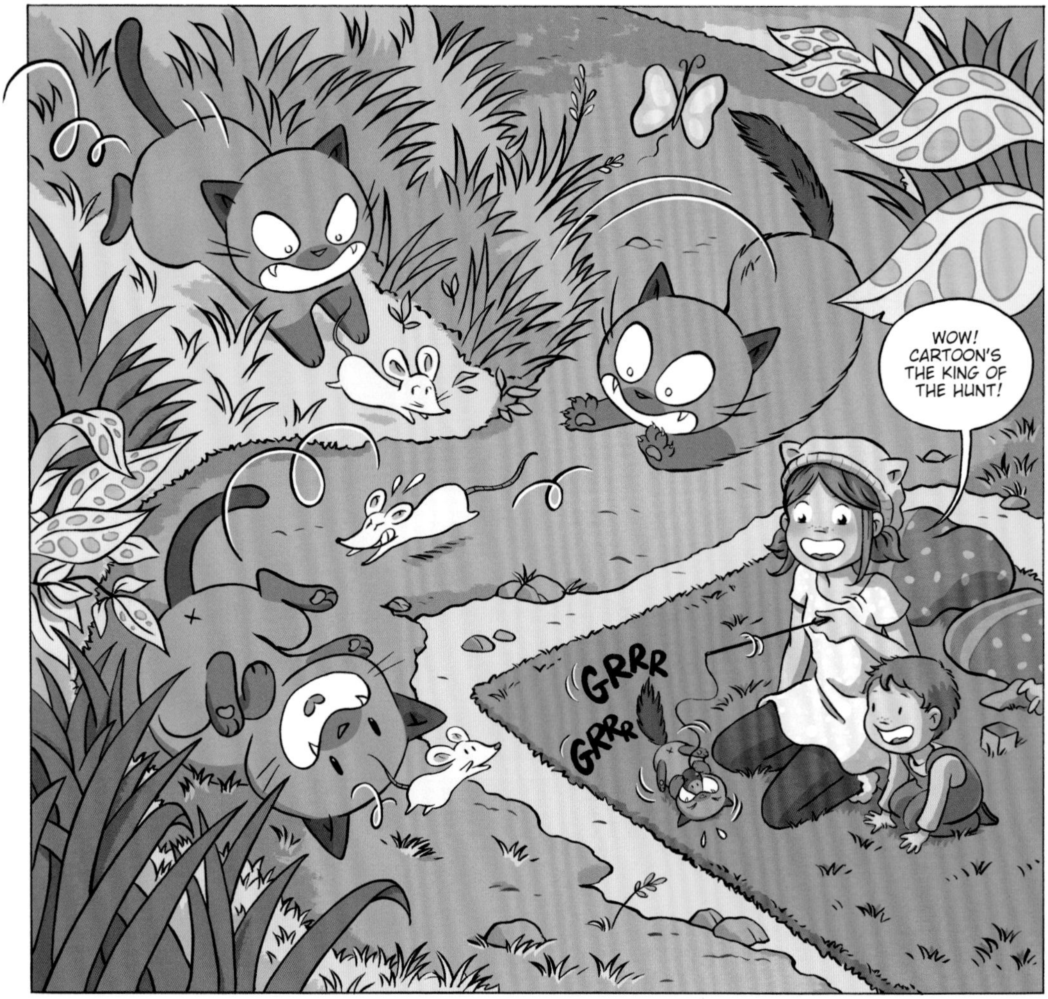
WOW! CARTOON'S THE KING OF THE HUNT!
GRRR
GRRR

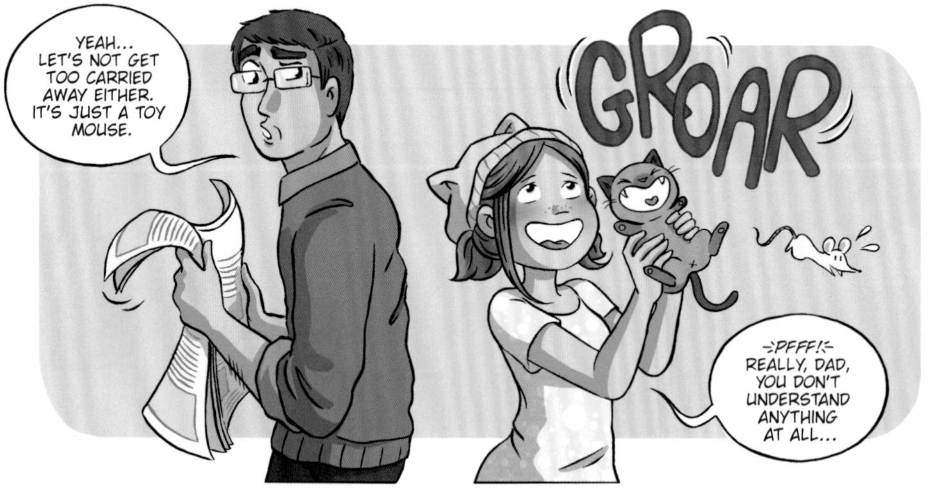
YEAH... LET'S NOT GET TOO CARRIED AWAY EITHER. IT'S JUST A TOY MOUSE.
GROAR
-PFFF!- REALLY, DAD, YOU DON'T UNDERSTAND ANYTHING AT ALL...

Gym Fitness

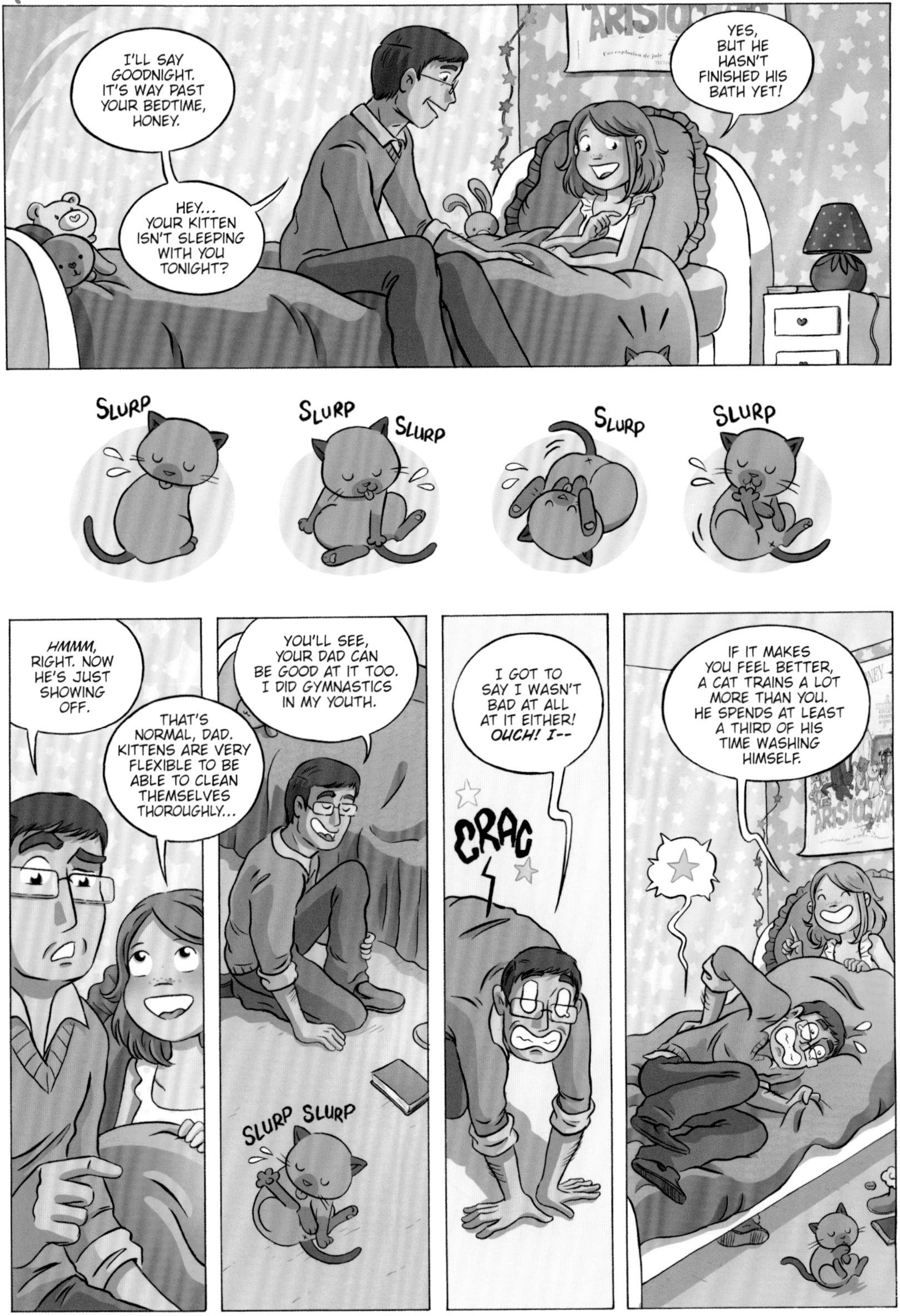

I'LL SAY GOODNIGHT. IT'S WAY PAST YOUR BEDTIME, HONEY.
HEY... YOUR KITTEN ISN'T SLEEPING WITH YOU TONIGHT?
YES, BUT HE HASN'T FINISHED HIS BATH YET!
SLURP
SLURP
SLURP
SLURP
SLURP
HMMM, RIGHT. NOW HE'S JUST SHOWING OFF.
THAT'S NORMAL, DAD. KITTENS ARE VERY FLEXIBLE TO BE ABLE TO CLEAN THEMSELVES THOROUGHLY...
YOU'LL SEE, YOUR DAD CAN BE GOOD AT IT TOO. I DID GYMNASTICS IN MY YOUTH.
SLURP SLURP
I GOT TO SAY I WASN'T BAD AT ALL AT IT EITHER! OUCH! I--
CRAC
IF IT MAKES YOU FEEL BETTER, A CAT TRAINS A LOT MORE THAN YOU. HE SPENDS AT LEAST A THIRD OF HIS TIME WASHING HIMSELF.

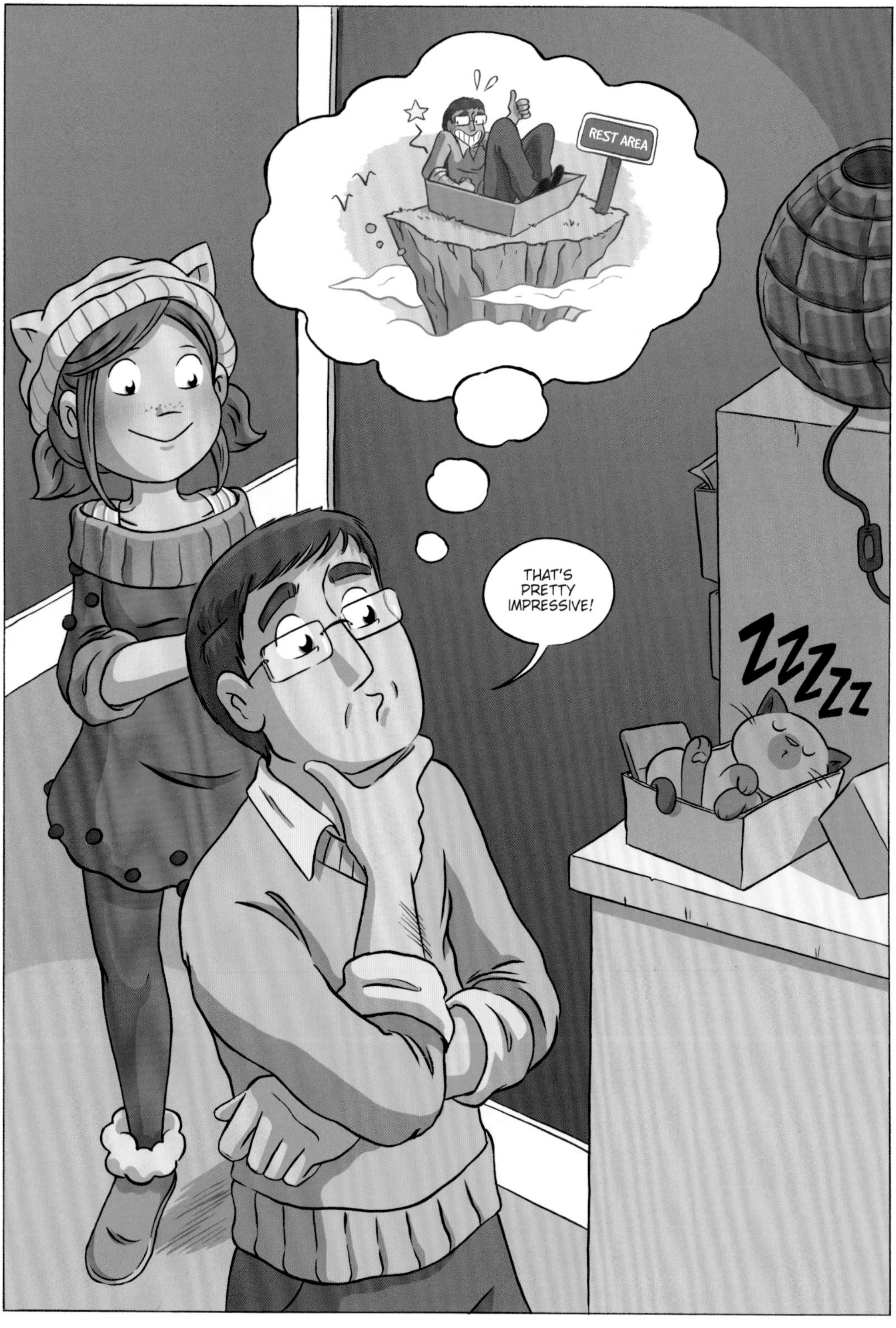
REST AREA
THAT'S PRETTY IMPRESSIVE!
ZZZZZ

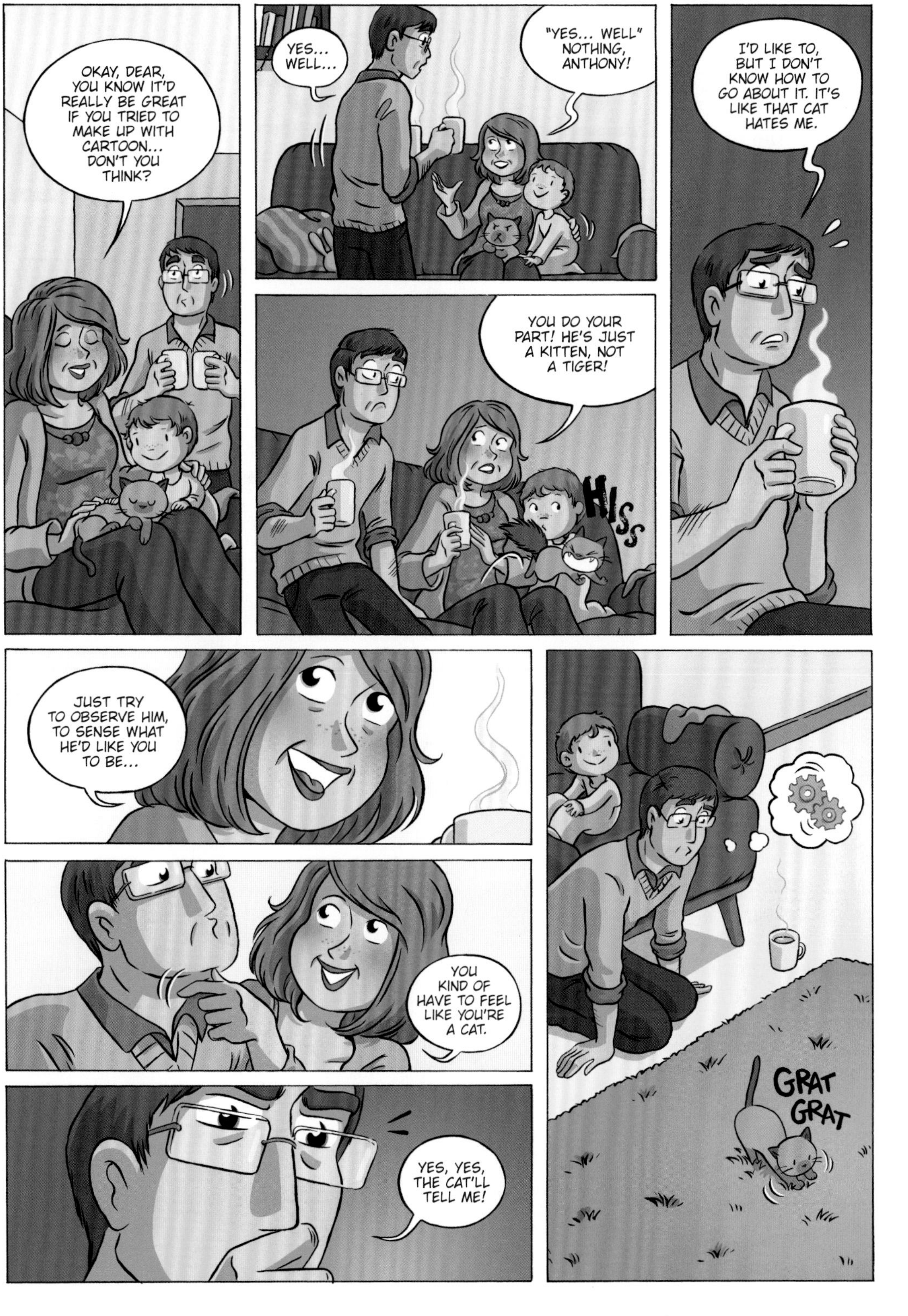
OKAY, DEAR, YOU KNOW IT'D REALLY BE GREAT IF YOU TRIED TO MAKE UP WITH CARTOON... DON'T YOU THINK?
YES... WELL...
"YES... WELL" NOTHING, ANTHONY!
YOU DO YOUR PART! HE'S JUST A KITTEN, NOT A TIGER!
HISS
I'D LIKE TO, BUT I DON'T KNOW HOW TO GO ABOUT IT. IT'S LIKE THAT CAT HATES ME.
JUST TRY TO OBSERVE HIM, TO SENSE WHAT HE'D LIKE YOU TO BE...
YOU KIND OF HAVE TO FEEL LIKE YOU'RE A CAT.
YES, YES, THE CAT'LL TELL ME!
GRAT GRAT

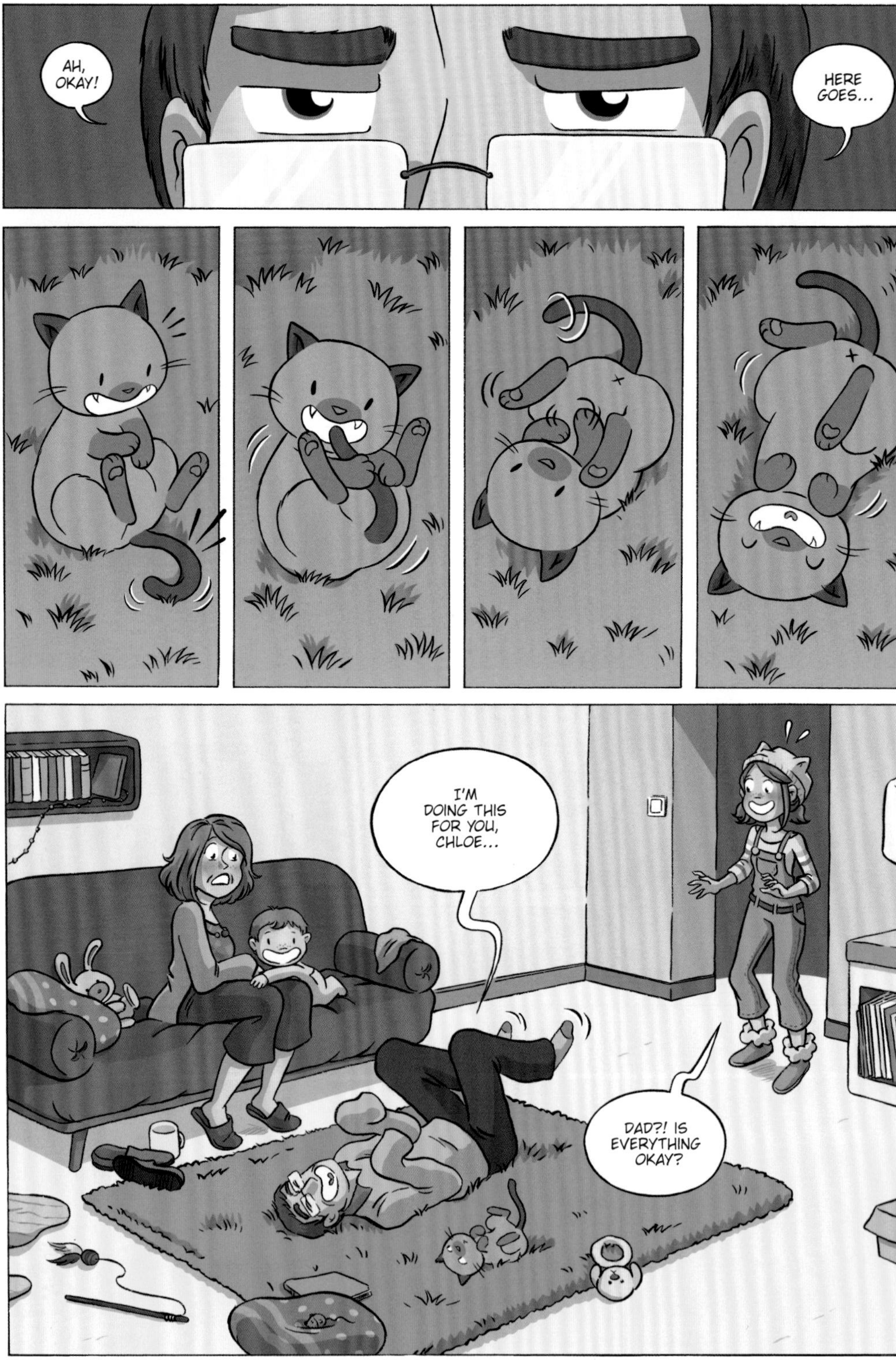
AH, OKAY!
HERE GOES...
I'M DOING THIS FOR YOU, CHLOE...
DAD?! IS EVERYTHING OKAY?

At Your Service

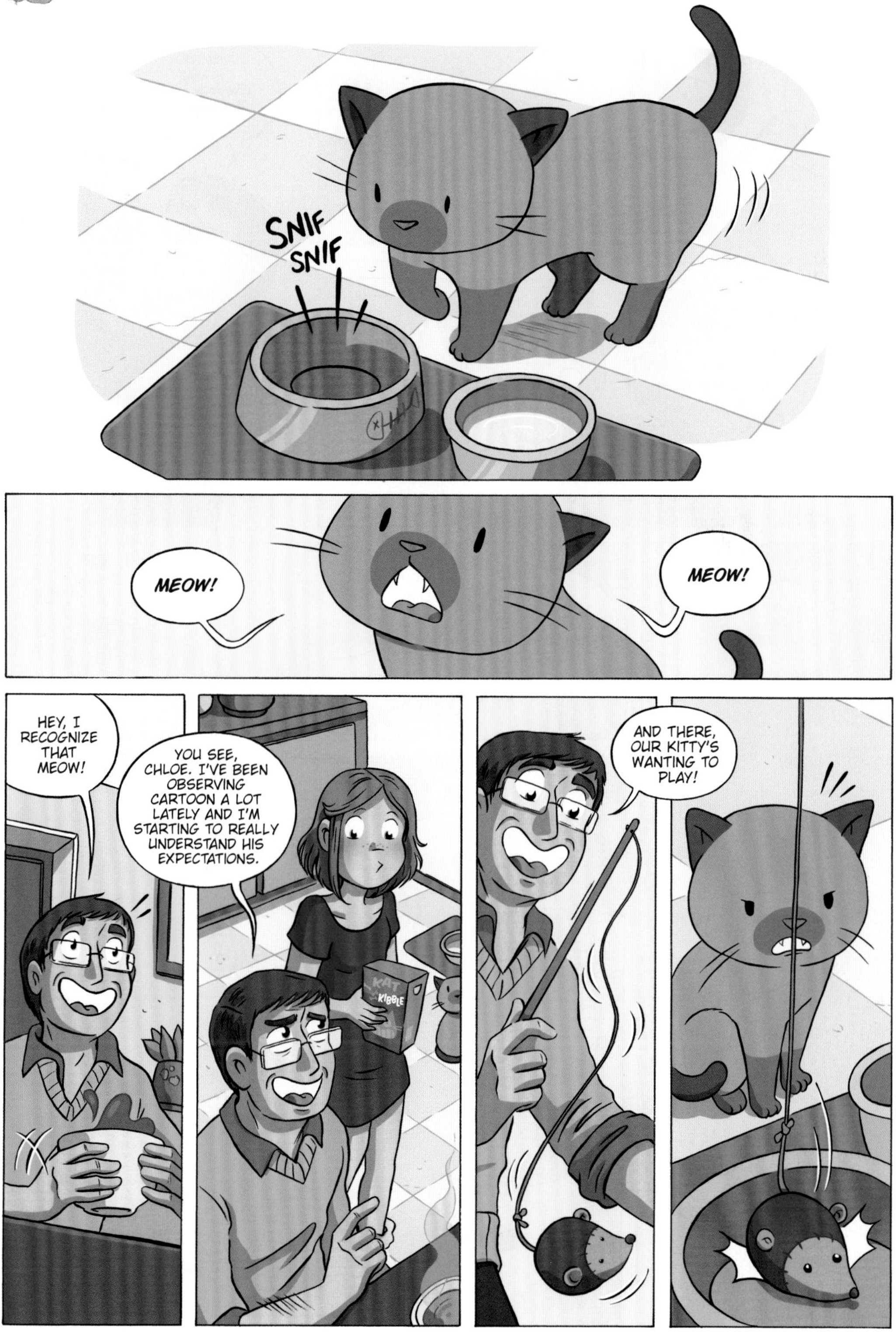
SNIF
SNIF
MEOW!
MEOW!
HEY, I RECOGNIZE THAT MEOW!
YOU SEE, CHLOE. I'VE BEEN OBSERVING CARTOON A LOT LATELY AND I'M STARTING TO REALLY UNDERSTAND HIS EXPECTATIONS.
KAT KIBBLE
AND THERE, OUR KITTY'S WANTING TO PLAY!

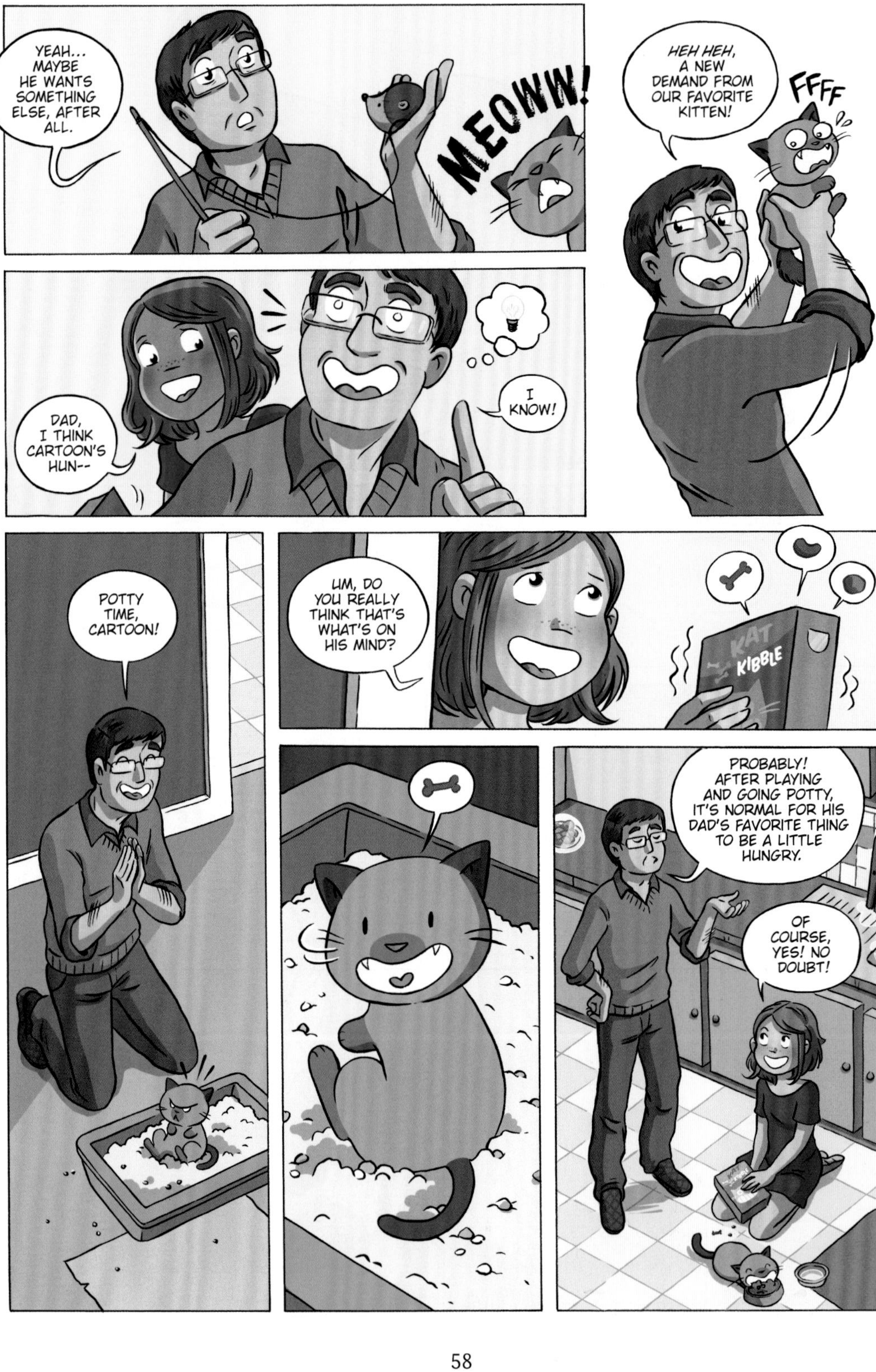
YEAH... MAYBE HE WANTS SOMETHING ELSE, AFTER ALL.
MEOWW!
HEH HEH, A NEW DEMAND FROM OUR FAVORITE KITTEN!
FFFF
DAD, I THINK CARTOON'S HUN--
I KNOW!
POTTY TIME, CARTOON!
UM, DO YOU REALLY THINK THAT'S WHAT'S ON HIS MIND?
KAT KIBBLE
PROBABLY! AFTER PLAYING AND GOING POTTY, IT'S NORMAL FOR HIS DAD'S FAVORITE THING TO BE A LITTLE HUNGRY.
OF COURSE, YES! NO DOUBT!

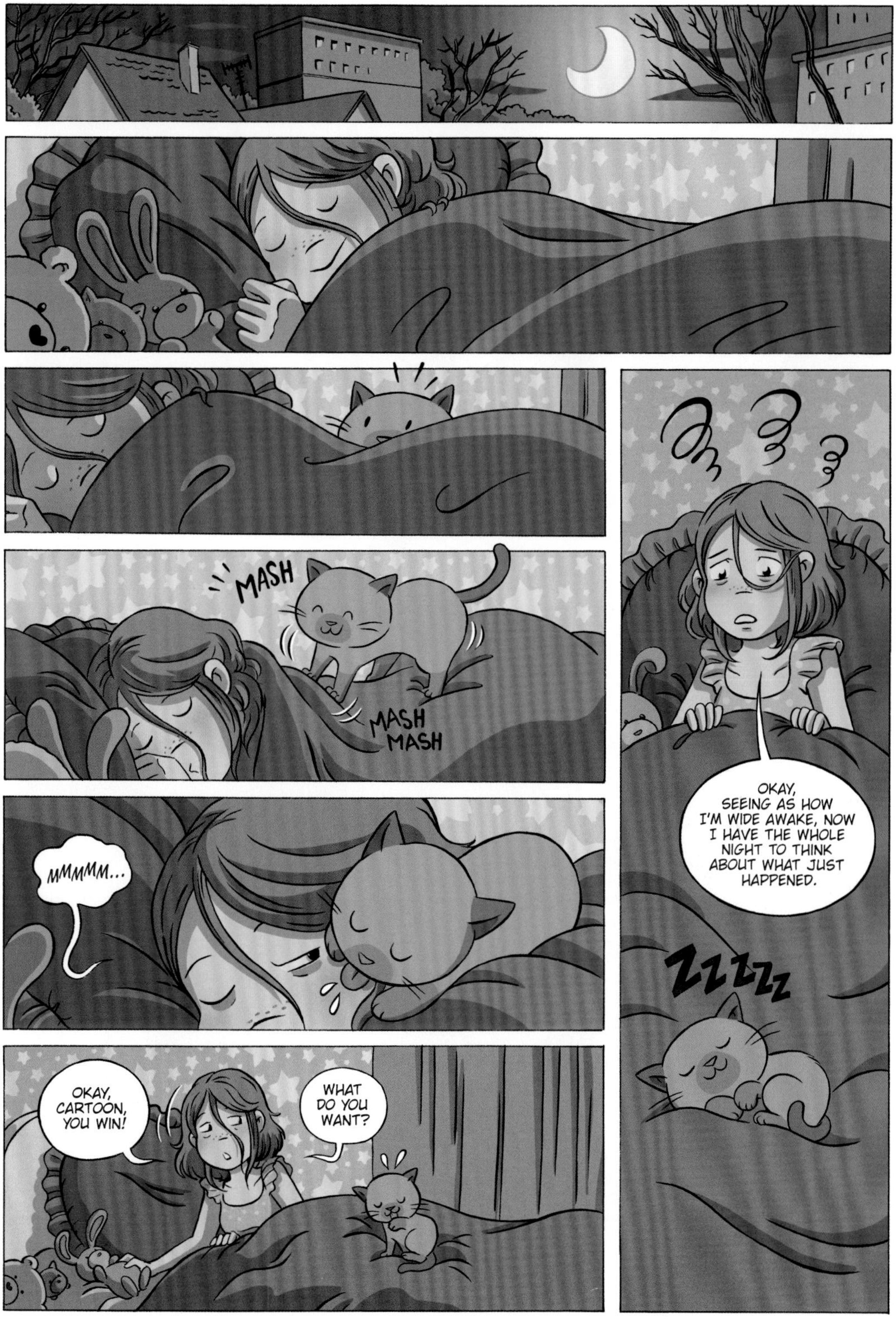
MASH
MASH
MASH
MMMMM...
OKAY, CARTOON, YOU WIN!
WHAT DO YOU WANT?
OKAY, SEEING AS HOW I'M WIDE AWAKE, NOW I HAVE THE WHOLE NIGHT TO THINK ABOUT WHAT JUST HAPPENED.
ZZZZZ

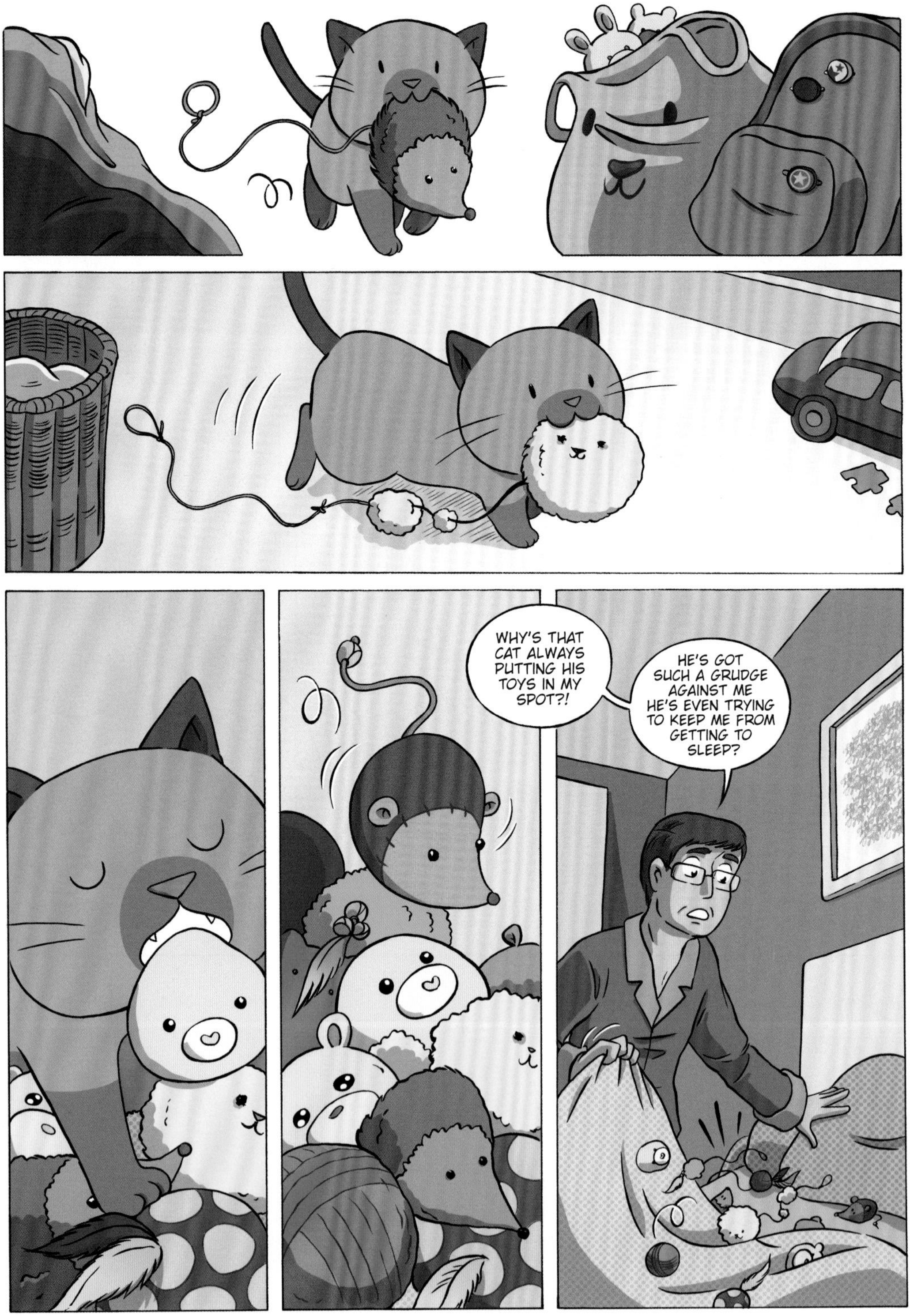
WHY'S THAT CAT ALWAYS PUTTING HIS TOYS IN MY SPOT?!
HE'S GOT SUCH A GRUDGE AGAINST ME HE'S EVEN TRYING TO KEEP ME FROM GETTING TO SLEEP?

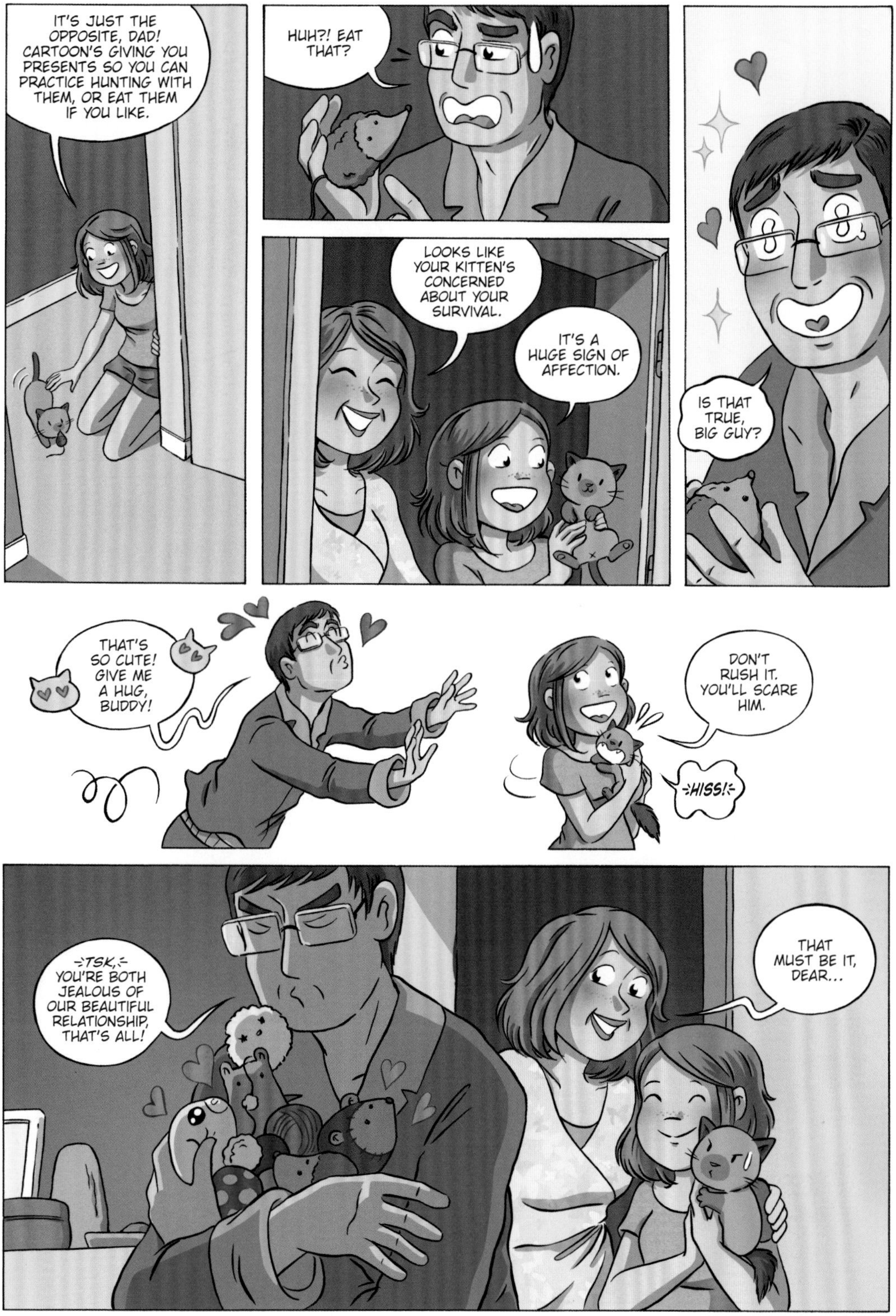
IT'S JUST THE OPPOSITE, DAD! CARTOON'S GIVING YOU PRESENTS SO YOU CAN PRACTICE HUNTING WITH THEM, OR EAT THEM IF YOU LIKE.
HUH?! EAT THAT?
LOOKS LIKE YOUR KITTEN'S CONCERNED ABOUT YOUR SURVIVAL.
IT'S A HUGE SIGN OF AFFECTION.
IS THAT TRUE, BIG GUY?
THAT'S SO CUTE! GIVE ME A HUG, BUDDY!
DON'T RUSH IT. YOU'LL SCARE HIM.
HISS!
TSK, YOU'RE BOTH JEALOUS OF OUR BEAUTIFUL RELATIONSHIP, THAT'S ALL!
THAT MUST BE IT, DEAR...

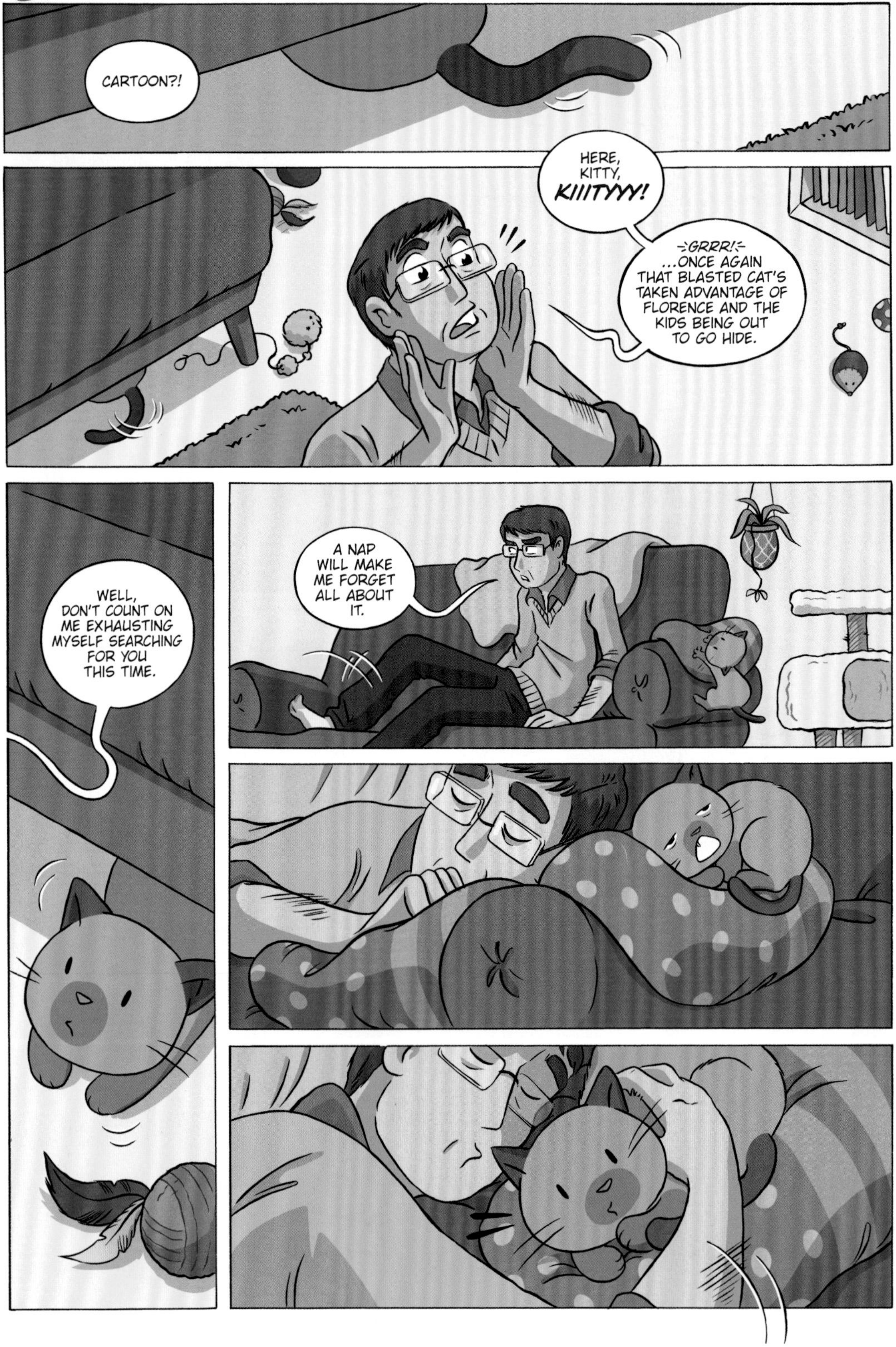
CARTOON?!
HERE, KITTY, KIIITYYY!
-GRRR!- ...ONCE AGAIN THAT BLASTED CAT'S TAKEN ADVANTAGE OF FLORENCE AND THE KIDS BEING OUT TO GO HIDE.
WELL, DON'T COUNT ON ME EXHAUSTING MYSELF SEARCHING FOR YOU THIS TIME.
A NAP WILL MAKE ME FORGET ALL ABOUT IT.

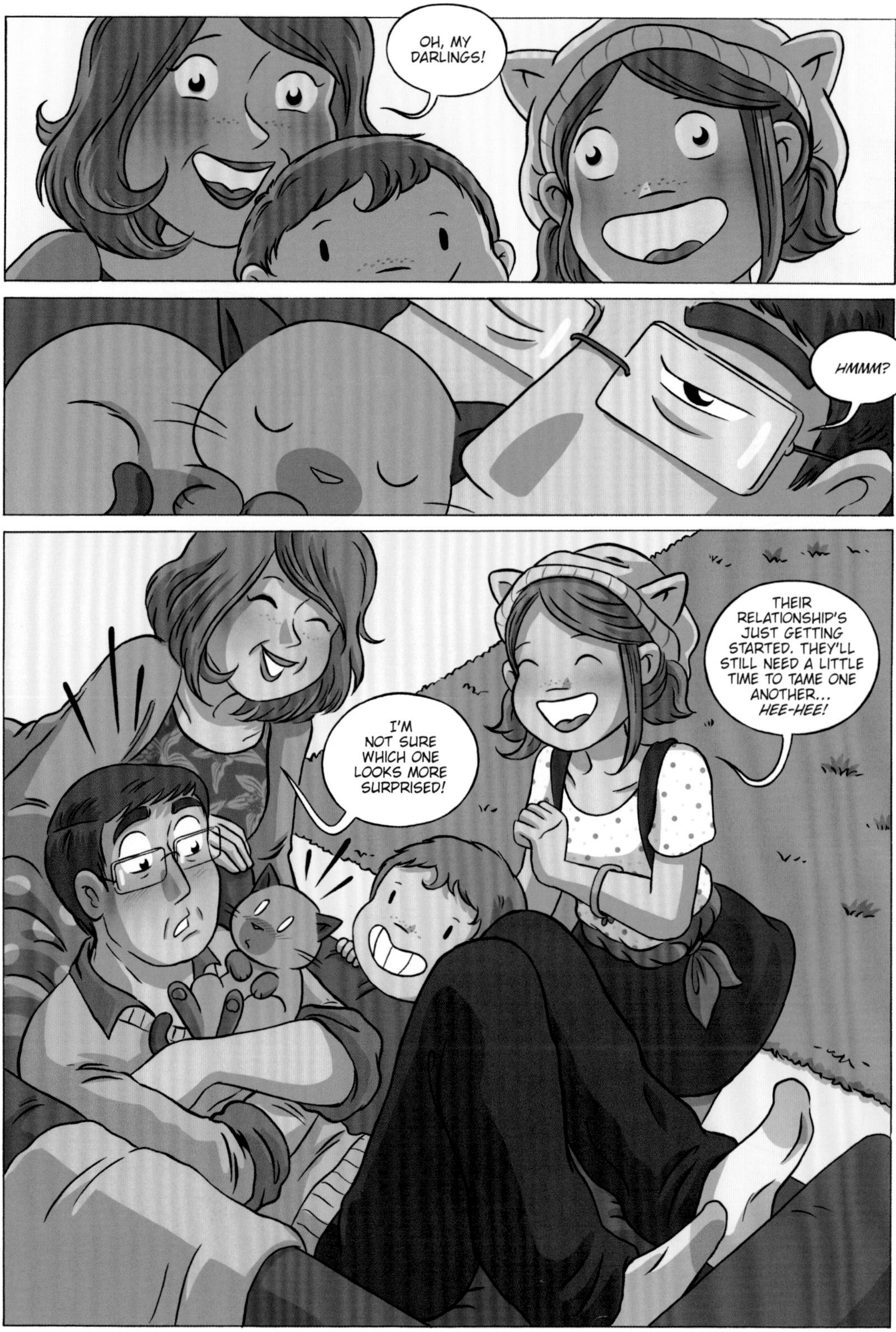
OH, MY DARLINGS!
HMMM?
I'M NOT SURE WHICH ONE LOOKS MORE SURPRISED!
THEIR RELATIONSHIP'S JUST GETTING STARTED. THEY'LL STILL NEED A LITTLE TIME TO TAME ONE ANOTHER... HEE-HEE!

tips from Chloe

Understanding a Kitten

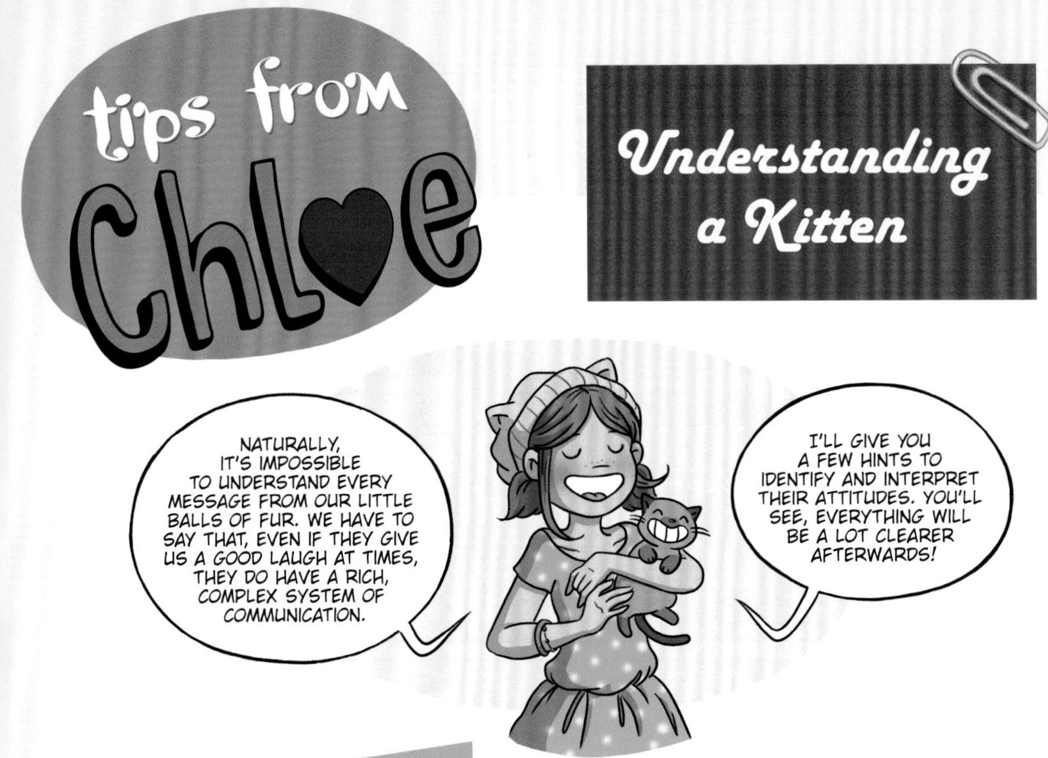
NATURALLY, IT'S IMPOSSIBLE TO UNDERSTAND EVERY MESSAGE FROM OUR LITTLE BALLS OF FUR. WE HAVE TO SAY THAT, EVEN IF THEY GIVE US A GOOD LAUGH AT TIMES, THEY DO HAVE A RICH, COMPLEX SYSTEM OF COMMUNICATION.
I'LL GIVE YOU A FEW HINTS TO IDENTIFY AND INTERPRET THEIR ATTITUDES. YOU'LL SEE, EVERYTHING WILL BE A LOT CLEARER AFTERWARDS!

Rubbing

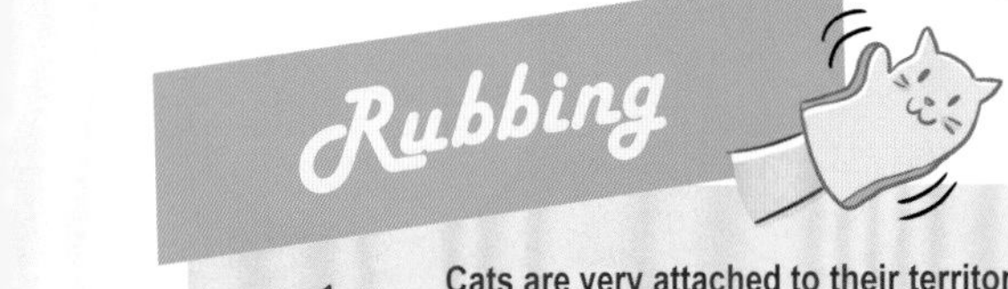

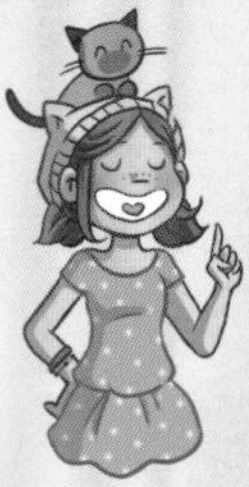

Cats are very attached to their territory. So, to show this is his home, he'll try to spread his odor throughout the different parts of the house. Aside from urine (your male cat will start to use this particularly effective trick around six to eight months of age), rubbing is the first way he'll leave his scent in order to indicate: "who I am," "the last time I came by here," and "what mood I'm in." Rest assured, afterwards, he'll feel like he's in a familiar, well-defined universe.

Conversely, not finding his markings will prove stressful, especially if there's a change of furniture or, worse, if you move.

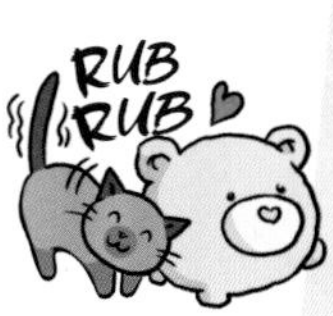
RUB RUB

A Bit of Advice:
If you have to travel with your four-legged friend, let him calmly rub his whiskers once he's arrived safe and sound.
Relaxation guaranteed!

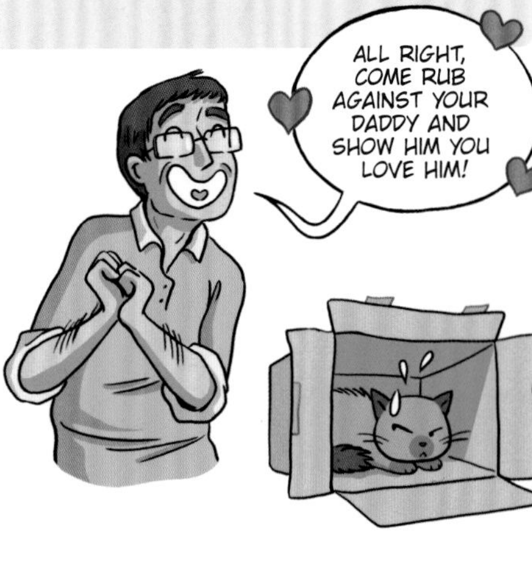
ALL RIGHT, COME RUB AGAINST YOUR DADDY AND SHOW HIM YOU LOVE HIM!

Good to Know: A cat's scent markers are also called pheromones. To pick them up, felines draw back their upper lip: it's called the flehmen response.

Scratching

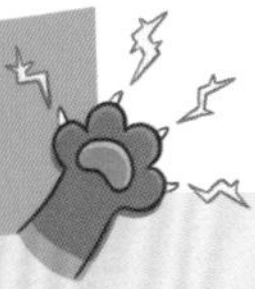

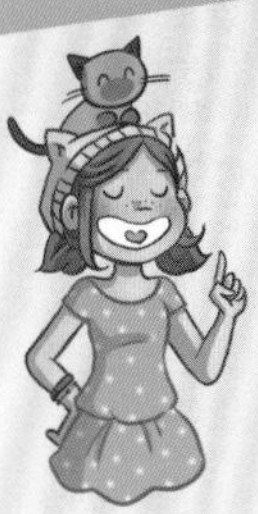

Scratching, which is usually from top to bottom, constitutes another form of territory marking for cats. In addition to being visible, these cuts let them lay down their scent markings in the places where they rest and pass through, thanks to substances secreted by glands located between their footpads.

This natural behavior is part of a cat's physical happiness: he also regularly takes advantage of it to stretch himself, to sharpen his claws, or also to get noticed. So, it's not good to stop him from doing it, but rather to manage it.

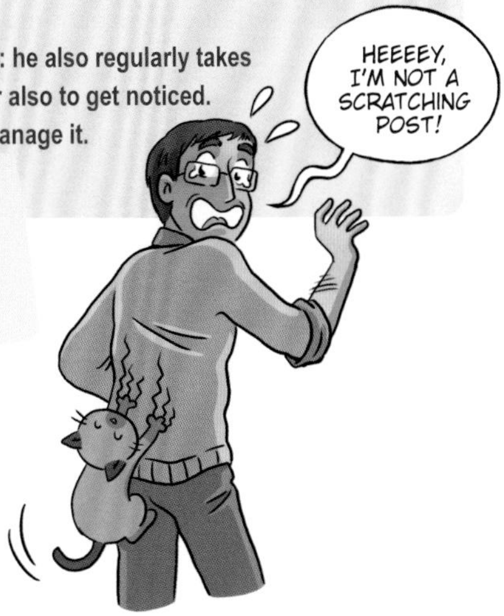
HEEEEY, I'M NOT A SCRATCHING POST!

A Bit of Advice: Your little friend's use of a scratching post or a cat tree essentially depends on its placement. Try, therefore, to put it in where your cat hangs out!

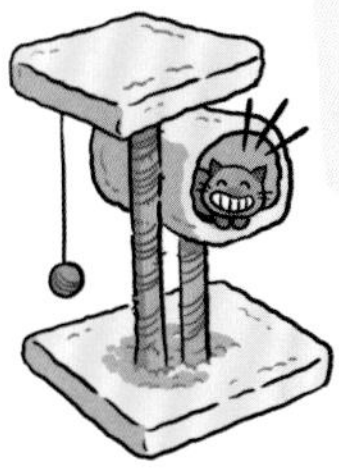

Good to Know: Your cat possesses five claws on each forepaw and four on each of the rear ones. The hind claws aren't as curved and sharp as the front ones.

Body Language

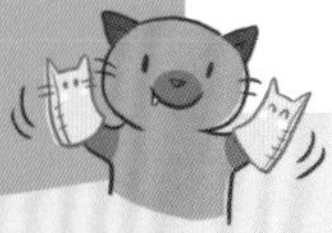

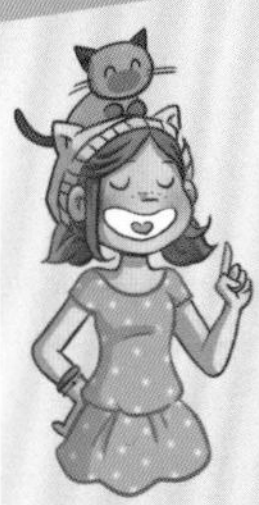

Since your kitten can't speak, his body language—through his posture or attitudes—is an invaluable indicator. The expressiveness of his tail can therefore be combined with the positions of his ears: laid back in case of fear or aggression, straight up or slightly forward to show interest. Lastly, a yawning cat isn't bored. On the contrary, with a cat, yawning is a sign of absolute relaxation.

With respect to a cat's grooming gestures, they represent signs of affection, whether it's by licking your fingers or face, or by nibbling your hair.

A Bit of Advice: If your cat lays on its back and shows you its belly, most of the time it means he trusts you and is asking to be petted.

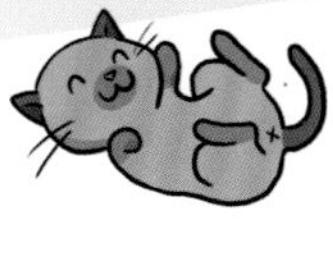

Good to Know: Your four-legged friend's body can move in every direction thanks to a large number of joints (his body has more bones than ours does), a very mobile spinal column, and an astonishing muscular system (he possesses more than 500 muscles).

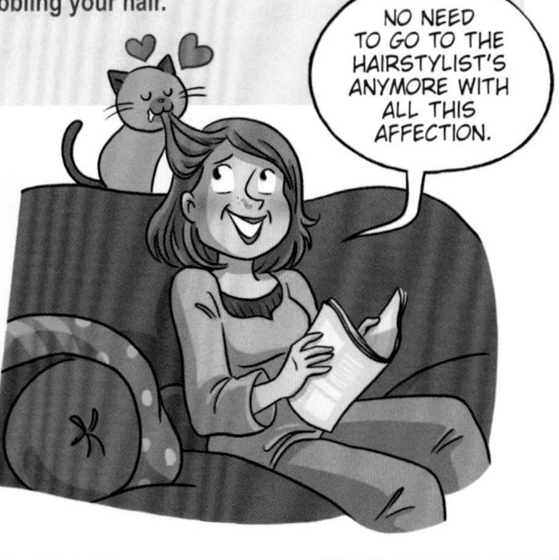
NO NEED TO GO TO THE HAIRSTYLIST'S ANYMORE WITH ALL THIS AFFECTION.

Meowing

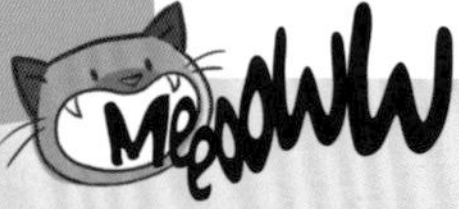

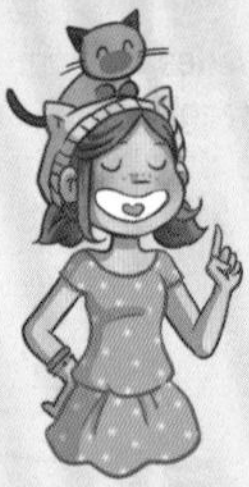

Peculiar to each cat (some are more talkative than others), meowing represents a demand for its companion. If you don't always understand to what circumstance it's linked, it will hiss or protest to itself depending on the case. Kittens possesses sixteen different ways of meowing, divided into "positive" and "negative" meows. Adult cats have nine.

Cats don't meow among themselves. They develop other kinds of vocalizations, like the battle cry of a male who's encountering a rival or the plaintive calls of the female when she's in heat or wants to attract tomcats.

A Bit of Advice: If your little ball of fur meows too often, it's because all his needs aren't being met. So, make sure you haven't forgotten something important like dry food, cat litter, or maybe just some petting!

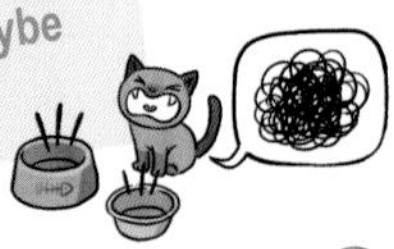

Good to Know: Cats also make sounds the human ear cannot perceive because they're beyond accessible wavelengths.

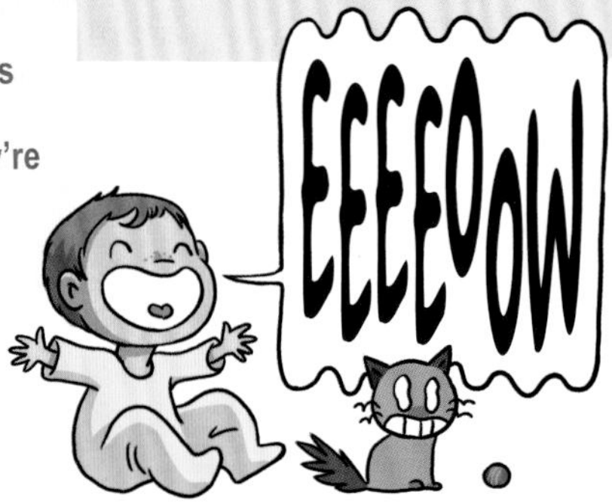
EEEEOW

Purring

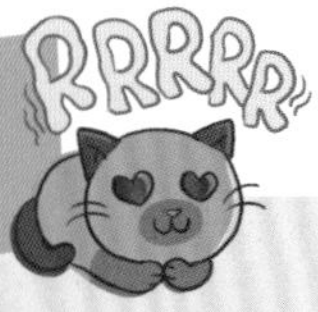
RRRRR

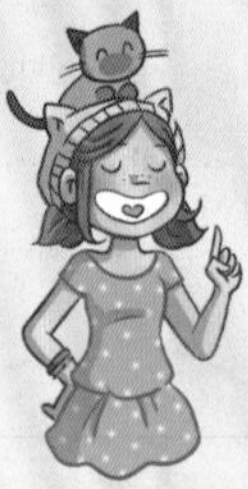

Even if it's sometimes associated with anxiety (your cat will purr then to reassure itself), purring is generally connected with pleasure. When your cat feels in harmony with you, he relaxes, and the machine gets started. So, a nice nap shared together or a good meal can be the occasion for him to express his contentment noisily.

These sounds that are particular to felines and recognizable among hundreds of noises come from the vibration of muscles located in the larynx and diaphragm. Frequencies vary according to the meaning of the purring.

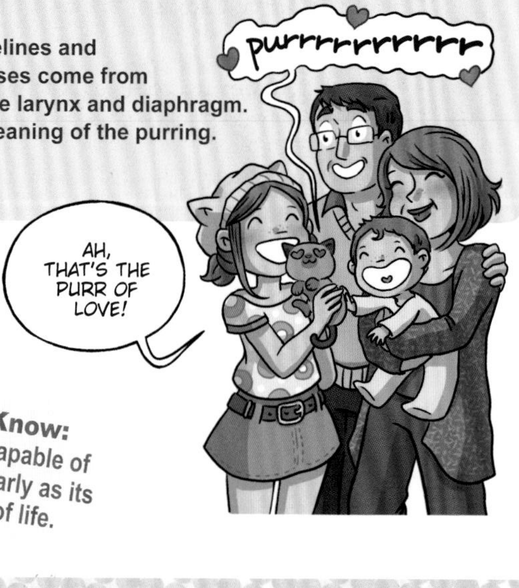
purrrrrrrrrr
AH, THAT'S THE PURR OF LOVE!

A bit of Advice: According to recent studies, purring causes a sensation of immediate relaxation in human beings. If you're stressed, don't hesitate to cuddle with your little four-legged friend or a friend's, or even go with your parents to a "cat bar."

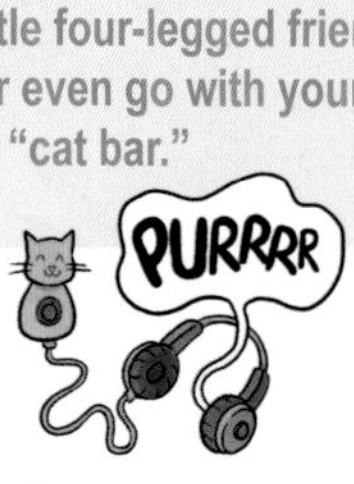
PURRRR

Good to Know: A kitten is capable of purring as early as its second day of life.

charmz chat

Welcome to the surprise CHLOE spin-off graphic novel, CHLOE & CARTOON #1 "When Chloe First Met Her Cat, Cartoon" by Greg Tessier, writer, and Amandine, artist, from Charmz, the romantic imprint from Papercutz, that cat crazy crew dedicated to publishing great graphic novels for all ages. (In case you're not familiar with CHLOE, it's the graphic novel series that features all the characters in this book, but just a few years older.) I'm Jim Salicrup, the Editor-in-Chief and Kitten-Wrangler, here to talk about cats. Seems that there are so many cats featured in Papercutz graphic novels, that it's often suggested that we change our name to *Papercatz*. Now it's spreading to Charmz! Obviously, we must love cats, with CHLOE & CARTOON simply being the latest addition to our feline line-up. Here's a list of some of the other cats you'll find published by Papercutz…

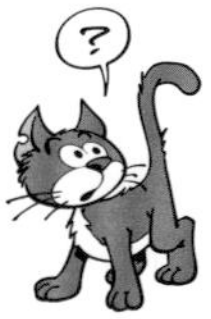
?

Azrael – This naughty kitty belongs to the Smurfs's archfoe, Gargamel. Azrael would love nothing better than to eat a Smurf! You can find Azrael in THE SMURFS graphic novels by Peyo (writer/artist).

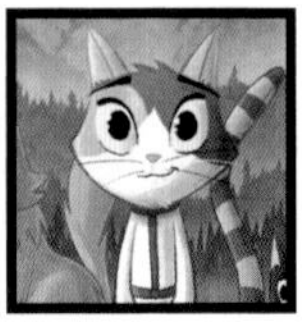

Brina – A two-year-old city cat, named Brina, takes a summer vacation in the country with her owners. Here she meets a group of stray cats who call themselves "The Gang of the Feline Sun," who convince her to run away with them and live life as a free cat. While Brina enjoys her newfound freedom and all the new delectable bugs the countryside has to offer, her young owners are distraught over losing her, someone they consider a member of their family. Brina is terribly conflicted and must choose to return to her owners or to continue to live free in the wild.

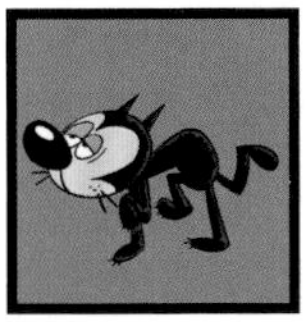

Cliff – Is the pet cat of the Loud family and is just one of the many occupants of THE LOUD HOUSE. There's Lincoln Loud, his ten sisters (Lori, Leni, Luna, Luan, Lynn, Lucy, Lisa, Lola, Lana, and Lily), his parents (Rita and Lynn Sr.), and the other pets, Charles (a dog), El Diablo (a snake), Hops (a frog), Walt (a bird), and Geo (a hamster). Cliff may not be the star of THE LOUD HOUSE, but the fact is that the Nickelodeon animated series is a big hit, as are the Papercutz graphic novels, so who's to say he's not a part of what's making THE LOUD HOUSE so successful?

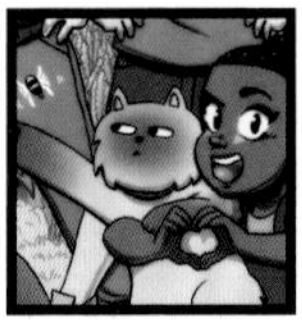

Hubble – Is the snarky pet cat of the Monroe family, and the unofficial mascot of the GEEKY F@B 5. Hubble has watched sisters Lucy and Marina Monroe, start up the Geeky F@b 5 with their friends, Zara, A.J., and Sofia, and tackle all sorts of problems, including finding homes for pets when the local animal shelter suffers major damage from a tornado. Even Hubble must admit that when girls stick together, anything is possible! Written by mother/daughter writing team, Liz & Lucy Lareau, and drawn by artist Ryan Jampole.

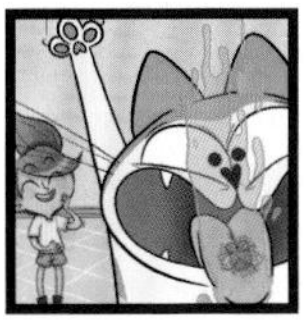

Sushi – In CAT AND CAT by Christophe Cazenove (co-writer), Herve Richez (co-writer), and Yrgane Ramon (artist), when Sushi is adopted by Cat (short for Catherine) and her dad, their quiet life of living alone is over. Between turning everything into either a personal scratching post or litter box, and the constant cat and mouse game of "love me/leave me alone," Sushi convinces Cat and her dad that they have a lot to learn about cats.

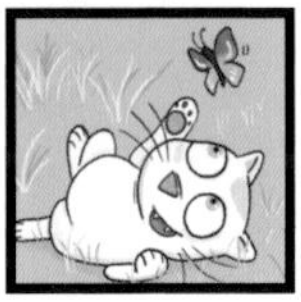

Sybil – Is the cute cat owned by fourteen-year-old (soon to be fifteen) Amy Von Brandt. Amy's life is never dull, and you can find out all about her and Sybil in AMY'S DIARY by Véronique Grisseaux (writer) and Laëtitia Ayné (artist), based on the novels by India Desjardins, and published by Charmz.

We could go on and on, but we think you get the point! (We didn't even mention Geronimo Stilton's purr-sistant foes, the Pirate Cats, who in the GERONIMO STILTON graphic novels, are always trying to rewrite history to their advantage!) Instead, we'll just ask you to keep an eye out for the next CHLOE & CARTOON graphic novel, and to watch out for Papercutz and Charmz!

Thanks,

Jim

Editor-in-Chief

STAY IN TOUCH!

EMAIL:	salicrup@papercutz.com
WEB:	Papercutz.com
TWITTER:	@papercutzgn
INSTAGRAM:	@papercutzgn
FACEBOOK:	PAPERCUTZGRAPHICNOVELS
FANMAIL:	**Charmz** 60 Broadway, Suite 700, East Wing, New York, NY 10038

Here's a special preview BRINA the CAT The Gang of the Feline Sun #1

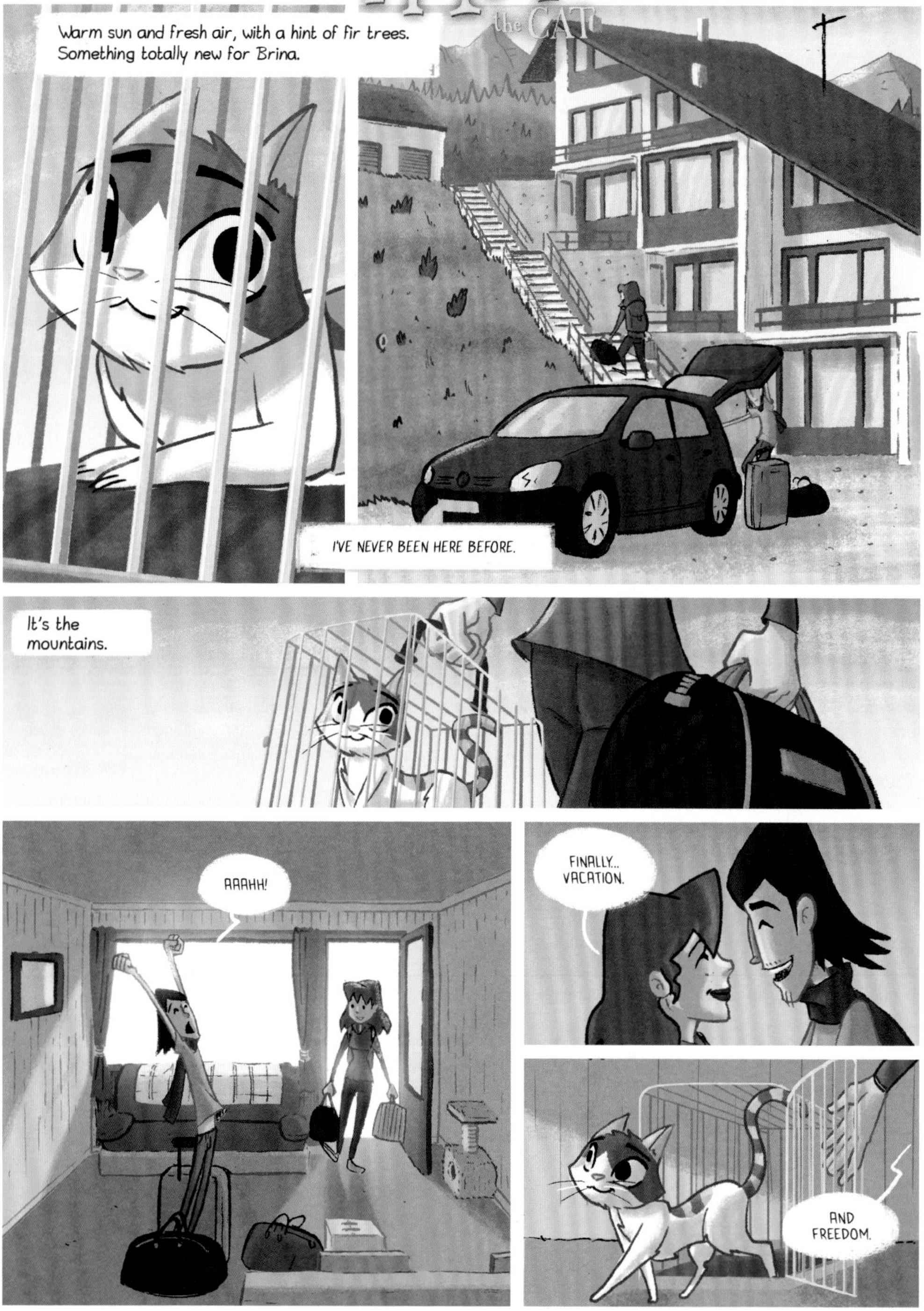
Warm sun and fresh air, with a hint of fir trees. Something totally new for Brina.
I'VE NEVER BEEN HERE BEFORE.
It's the mountains.
AAAHH!
FINALLY... VACATION.
AND FREEDOM.

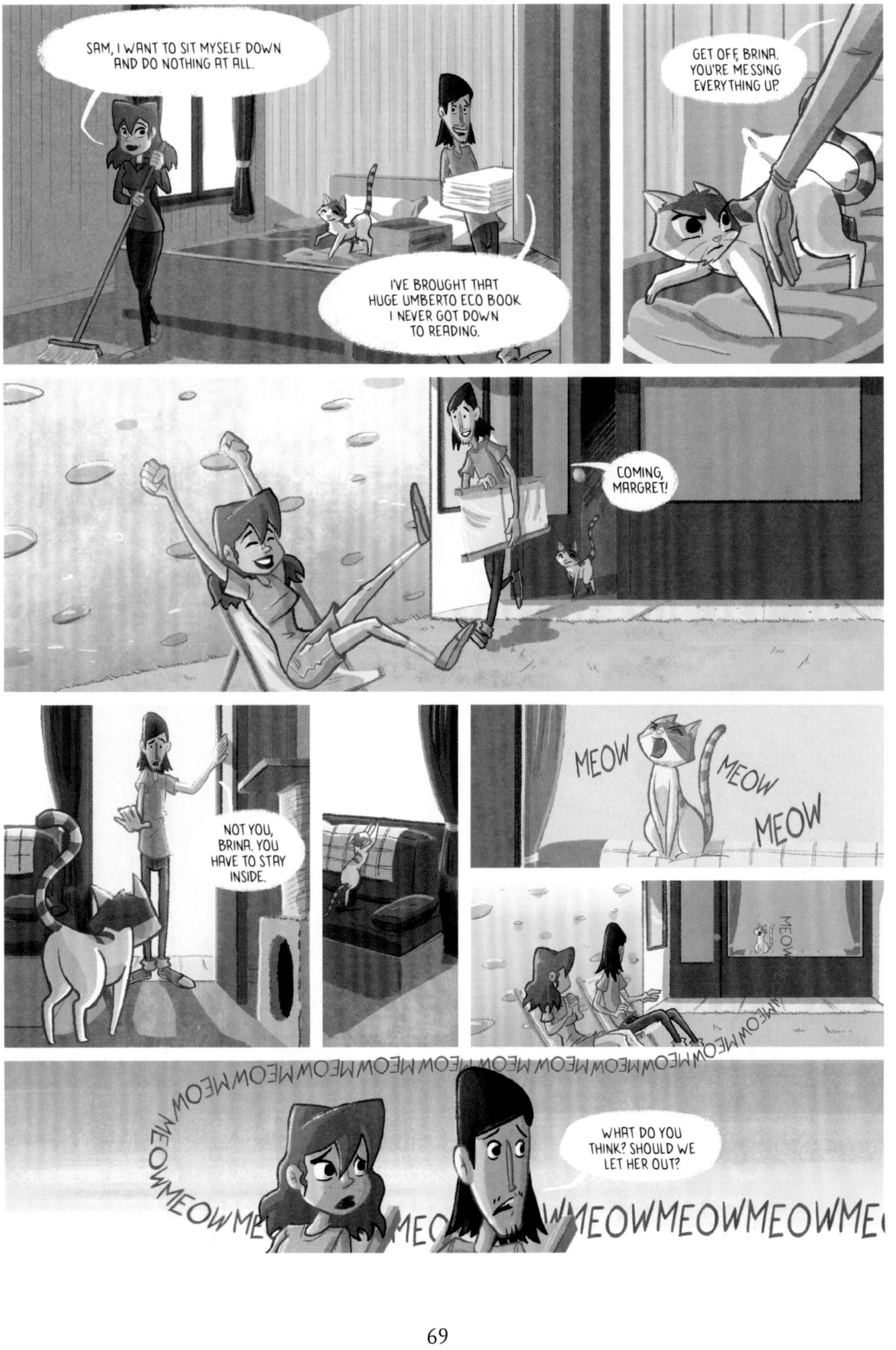
SAM, I WANT TO SIT MYSELF DOWN AND DO NOTHING AT ALL.
I'VE BROUGHT THAT HUGE UMBERTO ECO BOOK I NEVER GOT DOWN TO READING.
GET OFF, BRINA. YOU'RE MESSING EVERYTHING UP.
COMING, MARGRET!
NOT YOU, BRINA. YOU HAVE TO STAY INSIDE.
MEOW
MEOW
MEOW
MEOW
WHAT DO YOU THINK? SHOULD WE LET HER OUT?

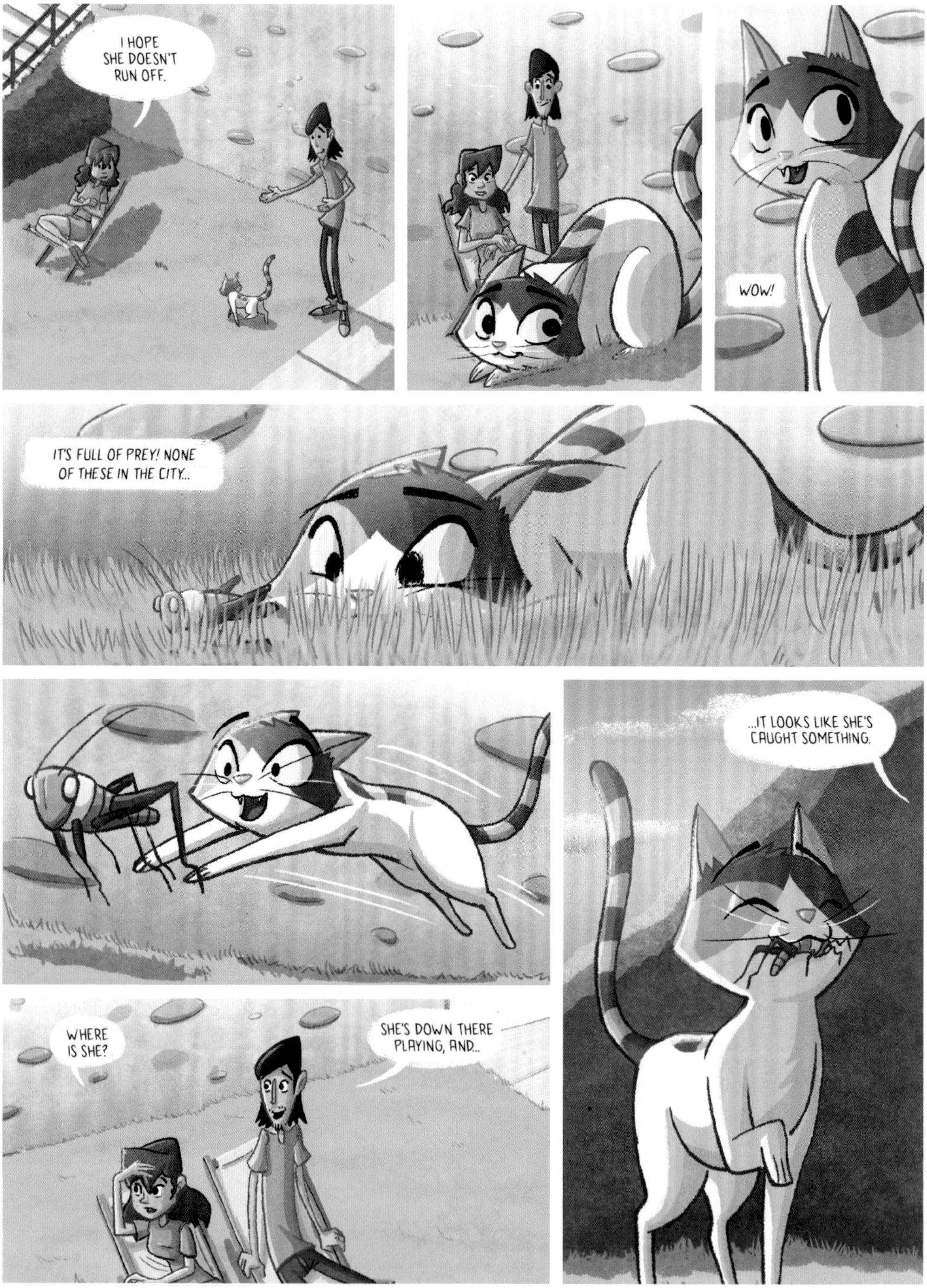
I HOPE SHE DOESN'T RUN OFF.
WOW!
IT'S FULL OF PREY! NONE OF THESE IN THE CITY...
WHERE IS SHE?
SHE'S DOWN THERE PLAYING, AND...
...IT LOOKS LIKE SHE'S CAUGHT SOMETHING.

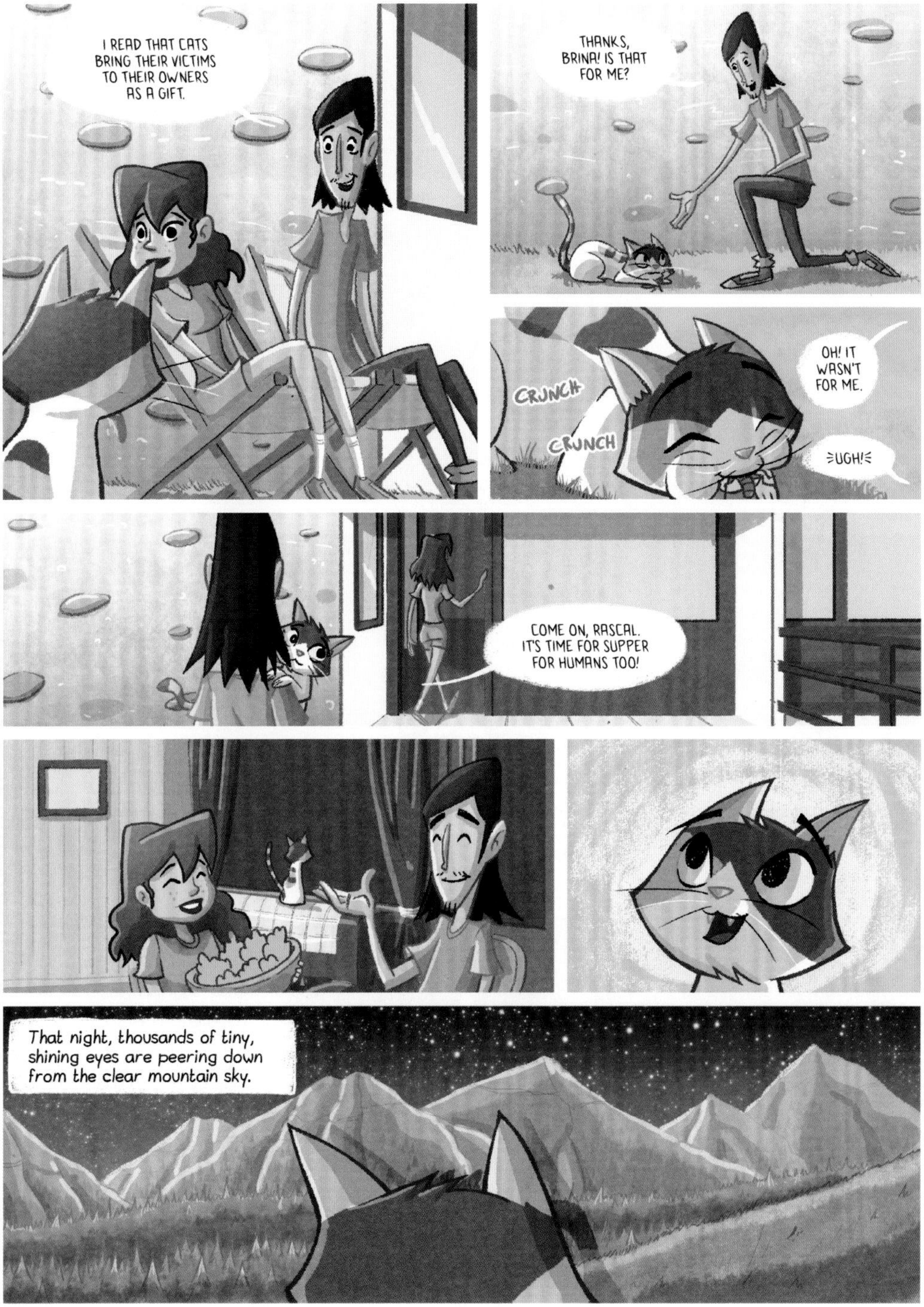
I READ THAT CATS BRING THEIR VICTIMS TO THEIR OWNERS AS A GIFT.
THANKS, BRINA! IS THAT FOR ME?
CRUNCH
CRUNCH
OH! IT WASN'T FOR ME.
UGH!
COME ON, RASCAL. IT'S TIME FOR SUPPER FOR HUMANS TOO!
That night, thousands of tiny, shining eyes are peering down from the clear mountain sky.

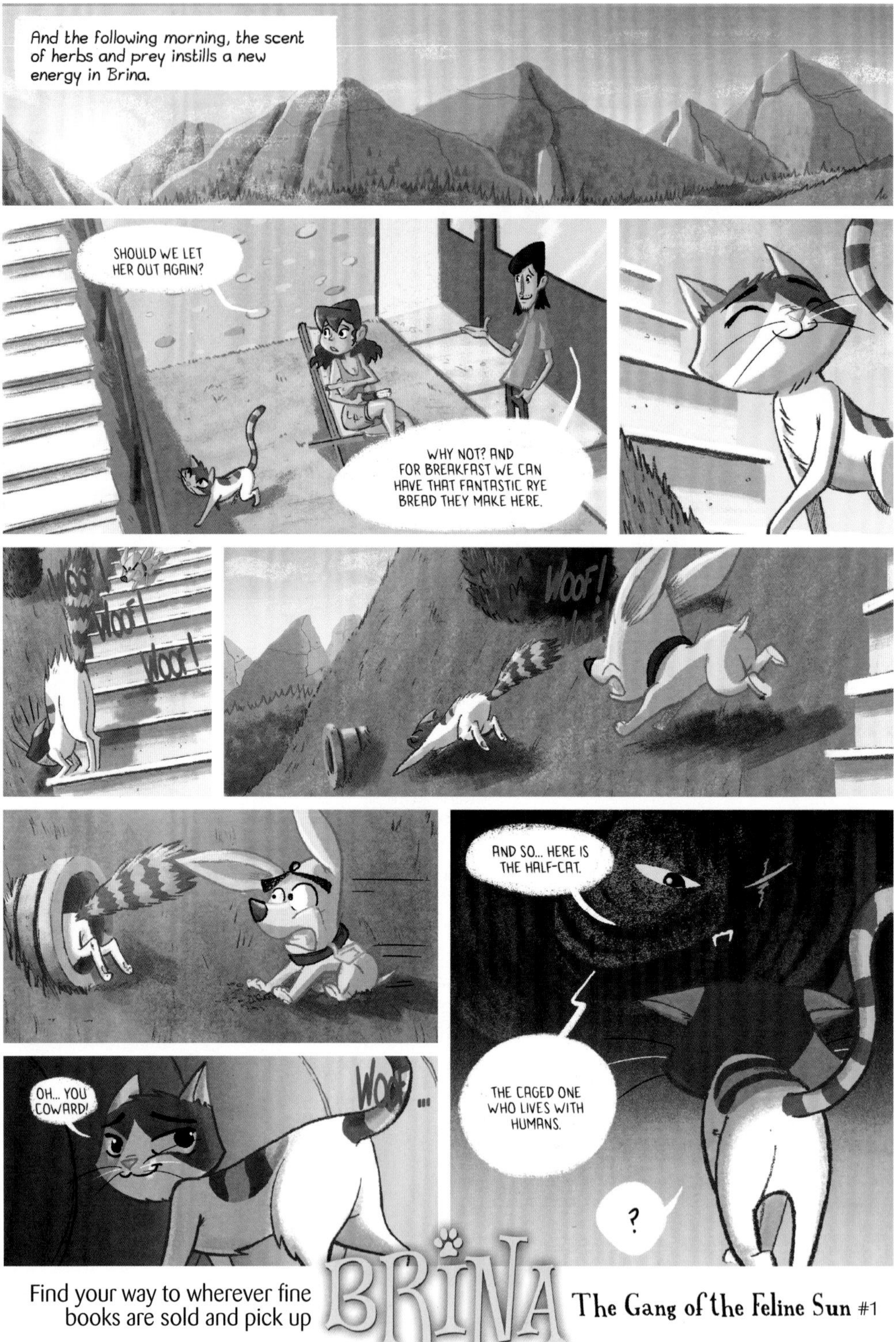
And the following morning, the scent of herbs and prey instills a new energy in Brina.
SHOULD WE LET HER OUT AGAIN?
WHY NOT? AND FOR BREAKFAST WE CAN HAVE THAT FANTASTIC RYE BREAD THEY MAKE HERE.
WOOF! WOOF! WOOF!
WOOF!
AND SO... HERE IS THE HALF-CAT.
THE CAGED ONE WHO LIVES WITH HUMANS.
?
OH... YOU COWARD!

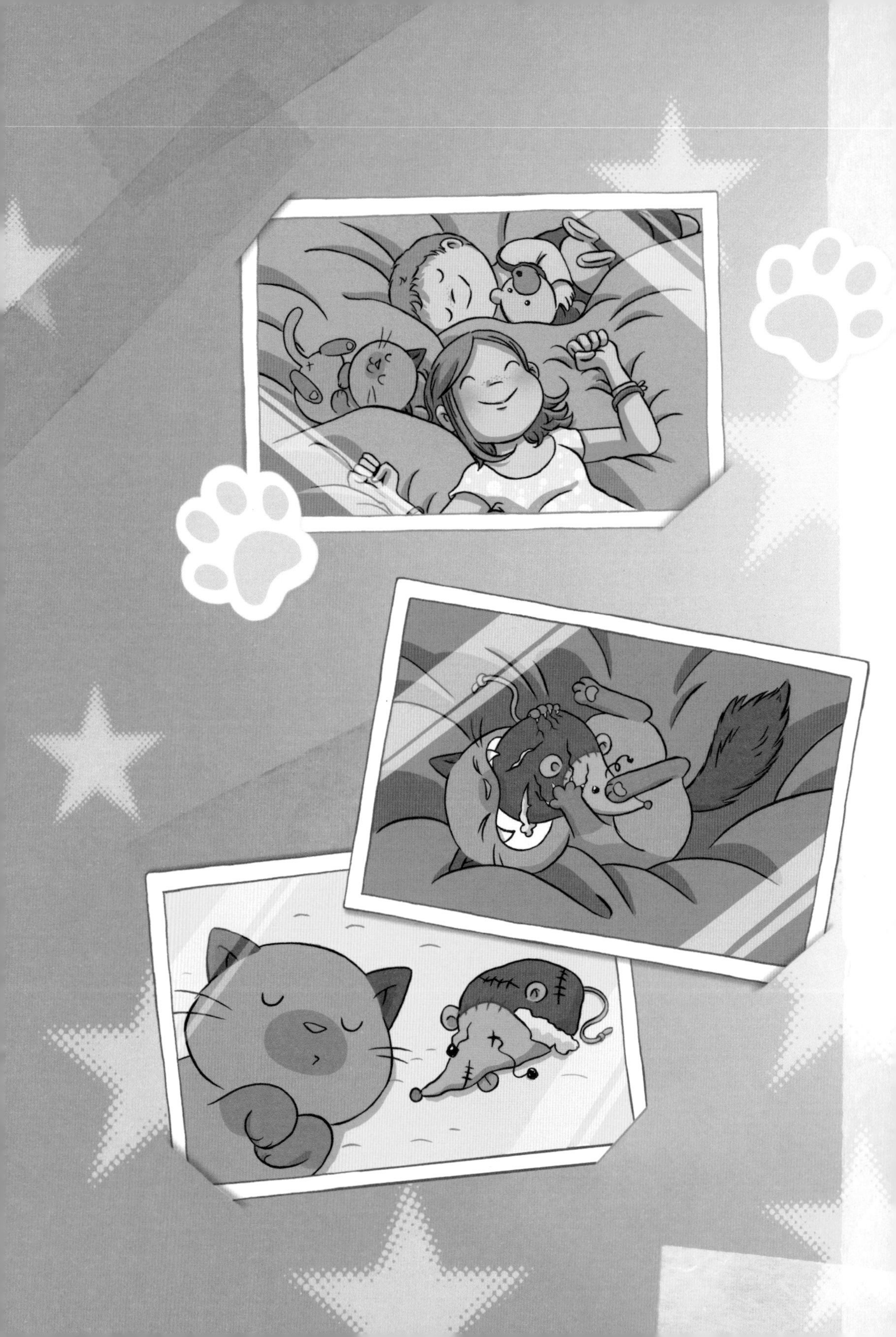